"Madam, your chariot awaits."

Gabe swept a theatrical bow, one hand extended toward her, a pure white rose held in his long fingers. "Its beauty pales before thine." He pressed one hand to his heart and gave her such a soulful look that laughter dried the tears trembling on her lashes.

She felt better suddenly. Somehow, it was hard to be afraid when Gabe was there.

"Allow me." He scooped her up in his arms, and Charity's eyes met his, only inches away.

Even more startling than the strength with which he held her was the sudden awareness she felt, a tingle that started in the pit of her stomach and worked its way up to catch in her throat.

For a moment, Gabe's arms tightened around her and she wondered if he felt it, too. Then his eyes dropped to her mouth and she felt the impact of that glance as if it were a kiss....

ABOUT THE AUTHOR

Dallas Schulze is a full-time writer who lives in Southern California with her husband and their Persian cats. An avid reader, she devours books by the boxful. In what little spare time she has, she enjoys doll collecting, old radio shows, classic and current movies, doll making, sewing, quilting and baking. One of her recent American Romances, *A Summer to Come Home,* was a finalist in the RITA awards for outstanding romance fiction.

Books by Dallas Schulze
HARLEQUIN AMERICAN ROMANCE

Don't miss any of our special offers. Write to us at the following address for information on our newest releases.

Harlequin Reader Service
P.O. Box 1397, Buffalo, NY 14240
Canadian address: P.O. Box 603,
Fort Erie, Ont. L2A 5X3

DALLAS SCHULZE

CHARITY'S ANGEL

Harlequin Books

TORONTO • NEW YORK • LONDON
AMSTERDAM • PARIS • SYDNEY • HAMBURG
STOCKHOLM • ATHENS • TOKYO • MILAN
MADRID • WARSAW • BUDAPEST • AUCKLAND

Published March 1992

ISBN 0-373-16430-0

CHARITY'S ANGEL

Chapter One

"Honestly, Charity, I don't understand you. You're twenty-five but you act more like you're ninety-five. Look at this place." Diane Williams made a sweeping gesture with one manicured hand, indicating her sister's living room.

"What's wrong with it?" Charity's eyes followed the gesture, seeking some fault.

"It's so...so...neat." Diane managed to infuse considerable distaste into the simple word.

"I like it neat," Charity said, not bothering to hide her smile. "After sharing a room with you for fifteen years, a little neatness is a pleasant change."

"A touch of untidiness is a sign of creativity," Diane said, picking up the old argument.

"Or the sign of a congenital idiot."

They grinned at each other, remembering all the times they'd said the same words with more acrimony. From the time Charity was born until Diane left home at twenty, the two sisters had shared a room.

Since they were as different as night and day, the arrangement had made for some memorable conflicts.

"I still say it's unnatural to keep everything so tidy." Diane reached for the pot of tea, pouring herself another cup.

"So I'm a freak of nature." Charity lifted her shoulders in a shrug, not visibly disturbed.

"You needn't think that I've forgotten the original topic," Diane said. She leaned forward and picked up another of the rich butter cookies Charity had bought specifically for her sister's visit.

Charity suppressed a sigh of envy as she watched Diane bite into it without the least concern about the calories she was consuming. It was one of the great injustices of the world that Diane ate like a stevedore and never gained an ounce.

"What topic?" Charity broke a cookie in half, with the vague thought that if you only ate it half at a time, there were fewer calories.

"Your love life."

"What love life?"

"Exactly my point." Diane finished the cookie and wiped her fingers on a napkin. "You don't have a love life."

"I'm perfectly content," Charity said, aware that it wasn't quite the truth. "Have another cookie." She pushed the tray closer, hoping to distract her sister.

But Diane was capable of eating and keeping to her point at the same time.

"You're twenty-five, Charity."

"I know. You keep saying that like it should mean something." She nibbled the second half of the cookie, wondering if the calories might somehow evaporate if she ate slowly enough.

"A quarter of a century," Diane reminded her ruthlessly.

Charity winced. "You do have a gift for a flattering phrase."

"I'm not trying to be flattering. I'm trying to get you to wake up and smell the coffee before it's too late."

"Too late? You sound like the maiden aunt in a Victorian novel. Are you about to tell me that I'm in danger of being left on the shelf?" Charity resisted the temptation of another cookie and leaned back in her chair, cradling her teacup in her hands. "I thought you were a little more liberated than that. If marriage is the be-all and end-all, then why haven't you taken the plunge?"

"I'm not talking about marriage." Diane waved her hand dismissingly. "And don't think I couldn't have been married half a dozen times if I'd wanted."

"Half a dozen? Are you aware that there are bigamy laws in this country?"

"Don't try to distract me," Diane told her sternly, putting on her best older-sister expression—the one she rarely had a chance to use. "I'm worried about you."

"Don't be. I'm fine."

"You're not fine. You're…you're stagnant, like an old swamp or something."

"An old swamp? A quarter of a century?" Charity bit her lip against the urge to grin. "Really, Diane, you should be careful about flattering me like this."

"You can laugh if you want to," Diane said huffily, reaching for a cookie. "But you know I'm right. It's not natural that a young, beautiful woman like you never dates."

"I date," Charity protested.

"And I'm not talking about mercy dates with the grandsons of the little old ladies who live in this apartment building."

"They're not mercy dates."

"When was the last time you went out with a man?"

"Last week. Mrs. Willoby's grandson. And he was a perfectly nice man."

"Could he get a cab in the rain? Order a wine? Did he make you feel special?"

"It was a friendly date, not the prelude to an affair," Charity told her, shifting restlessly. "And it wasn't raining and we didn't have wine."

"I'll bet he was either tall, skinny and tongue-tied or short, stout and never stopped talking about himself. He had moist hands and acne scars. He took you to some hole-in-the-wall place where they keep the lights low so you won't be able to look at the food too closely. He either overtipped or undertipped and he either made a clumsy pass or didn't have the slightest idea of how to make a pass if he'd wanted to."

"He didn't have acne scars," Charity mumbled, staring into her nearly empty cup. Why was it that Diane always showed these amazing bursts of insight just when you didn't need them?

"But I'm pretty close on the rest, right?" Diane fixed her sister with shrewd green eyes, reading the truth in her silence. "You deserve better."

"It's easy for you to talk. You're beautiful. You've got men falling all over themselves to meet you."

"You're hardly chopped liver. You're pretty."

"You know what Mom and Dad always said. Brian got the brains, you got the beauty and I got all the common sense."

"Well, they never meant that you were a dog, Char. I mean, people always comment on how much we look alike. You can't look like me and not be attractive."

It was said without arrogance. Diane Williams had spent the past ten years near the top of the modeling field. She was a stunningly beautiful woman, and it would have been false modesty to pretend she didn't know it.

Charity studied her older sister, trying to place just what it was that set the two of them so far apart when it came to looks.

They were both blond, but where Diane's hair was a miraculous pale gold, Charity's was more of a honey shade. They both had green eyes. But Diane's were electric, heart-stopping green. Charity's were a softer, darker shade. They'd both been blessed with dark brows and lashes but Diane's brows had a natural, elegant curve and her lashes were thicker and longer.

Their short straight noses were nearly identical. In her more desperate teenage moments, Charity had managed to convince herself that she had Diane beat in the nose department. Diane's nose had the faintest bump, a reminder of the time she'd fallen out of a tree and broken it. But somehow the tiny imperfection only emphasized the symmetry of her features.

Diane's mouth was wide, but Charity's was just a fraction wider. And of course there was the fact that when the tall gene was handed out, Charity had been sleeping in the back of the room. Diane was a willowy five foot nine. Her younger sister was a far-from-willowy five feet two and a quarter inches. And while Charity had never been ashamed of her figure, it always seemed just a little too lush next to Diane's elegant slenderness.

Charity sighed and reached for another cookie. The fact was she would never be the beauty Diane was. It had been the bane of her youth. Now it only brought an occasional sigh.

"Face it, Diane, I may look like you but there's some vital element missing."

"You can't tell me that you're so unattractive that men don't want to be seen with you."

"No, it's not that." Charity wondered how she could make her sister understand. "There's something very... motherly about me," she said gloomily.

"Motherly?" Diane widened her perfect green eyes. "You don't look a bit motherly."

"Well then, you explain why men always tell me their troubles. I've heard more stories of romances gone wrong than a therapist. Sometimes I feel like the *Statue of Liberty.*"

"The *Statue of Liberty?* You feel corroded?" Diane wrinkled her forehead, trying to find the connection.

"Not corroded. You know—bring me your tired, your poor. The huddled masses yearning to pour out their problems on some sucker's shoulder."

Diane's endearingly girlish giggle was one of the things that had always made it impossible to hate her. Charity picked up another cookie, biting into it morosely.

"It's easy for you to laugh. When was the last time a man took you out and told you how much he missed his ex-wife?"

"I can't say it's ever happened," Diane admitted. "But they can't all be that bad."

"Maybe not. But I've had it happen often enough that I've gotten a little leery of trying. Besides, I haven't even *met* a man who's interesting in ages."

"Well, there has to be someone you find attractive."

"You mean, besides Mel Gibson?"

"Come on, Char. You have to know somebody you'd like to date. Even working in that stodgy little jewelry store, you have to have met somebody."

"Nobody." But even as she said it, an image popped into her mind. Diane jumped on the quick flicker of expression.

"Who? Who is it? Come on, I'm your sister. You're supposed to confide in me." She leaned forward, her eyes sparkling with interest.

"There is a guy," Charity said reluctantly. "But I don't really *know* him. He's a customer, that's all."

"It's as good a start as any. You should ask him out."

"What!" Charity straightened so fast that tea slopped out of her cup and into the saucer. She fixed her older sister with a stunned gaze. "Are you crazy?"

"This is the nineties. Women don't have to wait for men to do the asking anymore."

"How many men have you asked out?" Charity asked suspiciously.

"Well, I would if I met someone I liked and he didn't ask me first. Besides, we're not talking about me. We're talking about you."

"I'm not asking Gabriel London for a date." The very thought made her feel as though she couldn't breathe.

"Gabriel." Diane rolled the name around on her tongue before giving a satisfied nod. "I like it."

"Good. *You* ask him for a date." Charity set her cup down with a sharp ping.

"I'm not the one who has the hots for him."

"I don't have 'the hots' for him," Charity protested, glaring at her sister.

"Sure you do. I recognize the look. Are you saying he isn't attractive?"

"Of course he's attractive. He's very attractive, which is precisely why I'm not going to ask him out."

"What? You only ask unattractive men out?"

"I don't ask *any* men out. And I don't care if it's unenlightened."

"We're only talking about asking him to lunch, not asking him to marry you," Diane said, secure in the knowledge that she'd never have to ask a man to do either one.

"Well, I'm not asking him anything except whether he wants to pay with a check or a credit card," Charity said flatly.

Diane shrugged, putting on an air of vague hurt. "Okay. It's your life."

"That's right. Have another cookie." Charity shoved the plate at her with a motion just short of violence, closing the topic.

Imagine suggesting that she ask a man out. Especially a man like Gabriel London. A man who probably didn't even notice that she was female. The idea was enough to make her break out in hives.

GABRIEL LONDON put his feet up on his desk, studying the toes of his rather worn boots. It was one of those rare moments when the station house was calm and quiet. There was nothing on his desk that couldn't wait five minutes, nowhere he had to go, nothing he had to do immediately.

He frowned at his boots, suddenly aware that the relative peace was not particularly welcome. The problem with peaceful moments was that there was nothing to do but think. And his thoughts lately had not been of the comfortable variety. He'd been thinking a lot about where his life was headed, and he wasn't sure he liked what he saw.

"Brooding again?" Annie Sarratt perched on the corner of his desk, giving him an amused look out of wide green eyes. "You remind me of..."

"Don't tell me I remind you of a chicken you had back in Alabama," Gabe interrupted her, giving her a frown that had no visible effect.

"You're thinkin' of *broody,* sugar. I said *brooding.* You know, sort of sulky. Pouty, maybe."

"You know, the reason I haven't asked for a different partner is because I don't think it would be right to inflict you on someone else," he told her.

Annie grinned. "The only reason you haven't asked for a different partner is you know you couldn't find anyone else who'd put up with your sulks, sugar."

She'd lived in California for fifteen years but her voice still held the slow drawl of the deep South. No one was ever going to mistake Annie for a Valley Girl.

"I wasn't sulking. I was thinking."

"The way you do it, there ain't much difference. So what're you sulking about now?"

Gabe poked her threateningly with the toe of his boot, hinting that she might like to go somewhere else. As usual Annie ignored him, shoving his feet out of the way to settle herself more comfortably on the corner of the desk. *His* desk, he noticed sourly. She never sat on the corner of *her* desk to harass him. Of course, that would have put her several feet away, which would have made it harder to really annoy him.

He looked at her through narrowed eyes. It never ceased to amaze him how such a delicate-looking little thing could be so tough. She was five foot five but looked smaller. Her skin was as pale and soft as a magnolia petal. Annie would never be found sunning herself on the beach. She didn't want skin like an old saddle, she'd say in that soft Dixie drawl.

She sat there wearing a slim little black skirt and a pale gray blouse, looking as if she should be off to a luncheon where the topic of conversation might be how to raise money for the local symphony. But she was one of the best cops on the force. In a tense situation there was no one Gabe would rather have at his back.

They'd worked together for six years now, and the only time he'd seen Annie lose her cool was when her husband had been badly injured in a freeway pileup. Other than that, nothing seemed to faze her, not gun-toting teenagers, belligerent drunks or family disputes, which could be as dangerous as anything a police officer had to face.

In six years they'd developed a mutual respect that had grown into friendship. He knew better than to treat her like an airhead, and she knew how to look behind the smile to his more serious side. But at the moment he didn't particularly feel like discussing his thoughts.

"How about we ditch this joint and find a cozy motel somewhere?" Gabe raised his eyebrows suggestively and gave her legs an exaggerated leer.

"I 'spose we could, sugar, but you know what a temper Bill has. He just might take it amiss, if he found out the two of us had been keeping company in a motel. I'd hate for him to have to break you in two."

"For a moment in your arms, I'd take the risk." Gabe pressed a hand to his chest, giving her his best soulful look.

Annie giggled. "You could take that act on the road, Gabriel. But it don't wash with me. And you ain't distracting me from the subject at hand, either. You gonna tell me what you're sulking about?"

"You're a hard woman, Annie."

"I know. Now what's got you frowning?"

Gabe sighed and gave in. He knew Annie well enough to know that she wasn't going to give up. She was like a slim and very attractive bulldog. Once she'd latched hold of something, she just didn't let go.

"You ever think about where your life is going?"

"Sure do. I'm going to stay at this job another two years and then I'm going to quit and stay home and have me two or three babies. I'm going to eat lots of chocolates and shuffle around the house in slippers and a bathrobe and watch all the daytime soaps."

Gabe grinned, trying to imagine his meticulous, immaculate partner letting herself go to hell. More likely, she'd have her babies precisely on schedule, and by the time they were six weeks old, they'd be organized within an inch of their lives.

"I'd like to see that," he commented.

"Well, you hang around long enough and you will. But I don't think that plan is going to work for you," she added thoughtfully.

"Oh, I don't know. I could probably manage to become a slob as well as anyone."

"No. You'd either end up moping or you'd be fussing for something to do. That's the problem with you Yankees, you've never learned how to relax. The minute you don't have something to occupy every minute of your time, you start to brood."

"Are we back to that again?" Gabe rolled his eyes in exasperation. "I told you, I'm not brooding. I was just thinking."

"What about?"

"About the fact that I've been a cop for twelve years now."

"And a good one," Annie put in, nudging his knee with the toe of her pump.

"Twelve years and I don't see any difference out there. We're still arresting the same people for the same things. So what have I spent twelve years doing?"

"You've spent it being a damn good cop. You put away a few bad guys, helped a lot of people and made a difference in their lives."

"Yeah, right. I made a big difference in Danny Androte's life." He broke off, the words surprising him. He hadn't even been thinking about the old shooting. He'd thought he'd come to terms with it a long time ago.

"You stop that right now," Annie told him sternly. "That boy had a gun and he'd already shot a woman and was fixin' to shoot you. You did what you had to do."

"So the psychiatrist told me. But the psychiatrist wasn't the one who killed a sixteen-year-old kid." Memories darkened his eyes to muddy green. He shook his head. "Sixteen years old, Annie. He should have been playing basketball somewhere, not robbing a liquor store."

"You didn't put him where he was. He was the one who made the choice to rob that store. Would you be happier if he'd killed you?"

"Of course not." Gabe shoved back from the desk and stood up, pushing his hands into the pockets of his jeans. "The point is that he's dead."

"And you're not," Annie reminded him pragmatically. "You did the only thing you could."

"Maybe. I don't even know what made me think of that." Gabe stared down at his desk, the shooting flickering through his mind in stiff, jerky images, like a badly wound tape. He shook his head, dismissing the memories. "I got a letter from my dad yesterday."

"He still want you to come to Wyoming and play cowboy?"

"Yeah. The ranch is doing fairly well but he'd like to expand. Says he's getting too old to handle it on his own."

"You thinkin' about going?" Annie asked, watching his face.

"No. Not really." But his eyes weren't as sure as his words. He shrugged. "I haven't been on a horse since my last pony ride at the L.A. Fair when I was eight. Can you see me on a horse?"

"I think you'd look real cute. Sorta like a poor gal's John Travolta."

"You mean John Wayne?"

"No, I mean John Travolta. Sorta *Urban Cowboy* goes to Wyoming," she suggested with a grin.

"Thanks. If you're going to be insulting, you can get off my desk."

"Whatever you say, Gabriel." Annie slid off the desk with easy grace. "But if you were thinking about joining your daddy, I'd be the first to wish you well."

"Trying to get rid of me?" Gabe asked with a half smile.

"No. I'd just like to see a little sparkle in those nice eyes of yours. 'Sides, it might be kind of fun to break in a new partner. Get a little new blood in here." Annie's teasing smile didn't hide the concern in her eyes.

Gabe watched her leave the room, his thoughts a couple of thousand miles away. He'd only visited his father's ranch once in the five years since he'd bought it. But the wide-open spaces and the vast expanse of sky had lingered in his mind, like a glimpse of heaven.

On days when the city seemed as close to hell as he could imagine, he'd think about the deep silence of the ranch...the sharp scent of sagebrush when you brushed against it.

The phone on his desk jangled, shaking him out of his thoughts. He shook his head and reached for it. He must be going through an early mid-life crisis. He couldn't be seriously thinking about giving up his career and moving to Wyoming. It was just a phase he was going through. In a few weeks he'd have forgotten the whole idea.

Chapter Two

Charity started the day by sleeping through her alarm—something she *never* did. In the rush to get to work at something close to on time, she'd broken a fingernail, burned the toast she didn't have time to eat and unthinkingly grabbed the most uncomfortable pair of shoes she owned.

She smiled at the couple across the counter and resisted the urge to look at the clock, knowing it had been less than five minutes since she'd looked at it last. Trying to ease her cramped toes inside the pearl-gray pumps, she listened as the man explained that he and Rosemary were getting married, and he wanted the perfect engagement ring.

Ordinarily this was the part of her job that she liked best. She'd worked at Hoffman's Jewelry for three years, and while Diane might see it as a stodgy little store, Charity enjoyed the customers.

Today, however, she was distracted by her aching feet and her empty stomach. Having missed breakfast, it had been inevitable that she hadn't had a chance to grab more than a container of yogurt for lunch.

Not to mention that the conversation with Diane kept playing in her head. She wished her sister hadn't used the words *quarter of a century* to describe her age. It sounded so antique. In less than five years she'd be thirty, then forty would loom up faster than she knew, and then where would she be?

Charity set a tray of wedding and engagement rings on the counter, smiling at the young couple. Really, today of all days, she was in no mood to deal with happily engaged people. Especially when they looked so young that she had the feeling the groom's mother had had to drive them to the store.

Twenty-five wasn't that old, she told herself briskly. The prime of life.

Or the beginning of the downhill slide.

She suppressed a shudder as the bride-to-be reached for the gaudiest ring on the tray. A huge diamond surrounded by emeralds, it was one of the most tasteless pieces in the shop. So tasteless that it had been sitting in the case, unsold, for as long as she could remember.

Within half an hour the ring had been lovingly boxed and presented to the young man. Wasn't it fortunate that the ring just fit Rosemary's small hand, he'd said with a smitten glance at his fiancée. Personally Charity thought the ring looked like a cheap

Christmas ornament, but she kept the opinion to herself.

After Rosemary and her fiancé left, the store was momentarily without customers. Charity signaled to Sally, the only other employee, to take her break. With the manager, Al Kocek, hiding in the office, probably sleeping, and Sally on break, Charity was alone in the store.

She eased her right foot out of its shoe, sighing with relief as she flexed her cramped toes. Rubbing a polishing cloth idly over one of the glass cases, she found her thoughts drifting to the conversation she'd had with her sister the day before.

Maybe Diane was right. Maybe she *should* make an effort to get out more, to meet interesting men. But she'd have to do something about her image. She wasn't sure what it was that made men see her more as a sisterly confidante than a lover, but there had to be a way to change the picture.

Maybe she should try a red leather miniskirt. She could have her hair permed into wild curls and buy a pair of those huge dangling earrings that her brother always said looked like cheap fishing lures. Three-inch spikes to give her a little more height.

She narrowed her eyes, trying to bring the picture into focus, but all she saw was a short, well-rounded blonde who looked as if she was dressed for a Halloween party.

She sighed, dismissing the idea without regret. She might as well face it. She was never going to look like a femme fatale. She wasn't even going to look like a femme semi-fatale. She was cursed with a wholesome look, and she was just going to have to live with it.

It was easy for Diane to talk about getting out more. Men stumbled over themselves to take her out, and not to talk about their old girlfriends, either.

When the bell over the shop door pinged, she looked up, relieved to have her thoughts interrupted. When she saw who was entering, Charity felt her face grow warm. She slid her shoe back on, hardly noticing her pinched toes.

"Mr. London." She moved forward, trying to ignore the way her pulse skipped a beat when he smiled at her. She'd seen that wide smile in more than a few of her fantasies.

"Hi."

"We just got a new shipment of crystal last week," she said, stopping at the shelves near the front of the store where a series of delicate crystal creatures basked in the late-afternoon sun.

"I noticed. Let me see the Pegasus, would you?"

Charity handed him the small winged horse, oddly pleased that he'd chosen her favorite piece. He cupped it in his fingers, holding it up so that the sunlight poured through it. Charity studied him while he examined it.

It was odd how his face had come to mind while she was talking with Diane yesterday. It wasn't as if she really knew him, not on any personal level.

Gabriel London had been coming into Hoffman's for over a year. Every month or so he came in and bought one of the little crystal animals Mr. Hoffman imported from Europe. The small pieces were exquisitely crafted and priced accordingly. They had a number of customers who collected them but none who lingered in her thoughts like Gabriel London.

It was hard to say just what it was about him that made him so memorable. He wasn't enormously tall— an inch or so over six feet maybe. He was built on lean lines, all muscle and not much bulk.

His hair was medium brown, worn short but shaggy, as if he couldn't be bothered with keeping it tamed. His eyes were hazel, a rich amalgam of green and gold. His features were too long, too angular to be really handsome. His mouth was wide, bracketed by lines that said he smiled often. His chin was strong, stubbornly shaped. His nose was . . . well, rather noselike.

Nothing all that extraordinary. But somehow it all blended into a whole that was considerably greater than the sum of the parts. No mere physical catalog could capture the way his eyes wrinkled at the corners when he smiled. Or the way he moved with a sort of casual grace that made her heart beat just a little faster than it had any business doing.

"What do you think?"

Charity blinked. What did she think? She'd been so wrapped up in analyzing Gabriel London that for an instant she thought he was asking her opinion of himself.

"Think?"

"Of the Pegasus," he prompted.

"The Pegasus. Of course." She blinked at the small crystal figure in his hand, trying to shift her thinking.

"Mind on other things?" he asked.

"Just drifted off, I guess. Sorry."

"No problem. Daydreams are a sign of an intelligent mind."

"According to whom?"

"According to me," he said, giving her that grin that never failed to make her heart skip.

"I'm not sure my boss would buy that philosophy," she told him with a smile.

"A slave driver?" he asked sympathetically.

"No. But he's not much inclined to encourage daydreaming on the job."

"Too bad." He held the Pegasus up so that the sunlight streamed through it. The delicate wings seemed to quiver with life. If she narrowed her eyes, Charity could almost believe it was about to take flight.

"It looks alive, doesn't it," he said, reading her thoughts.

"Yes. It's a lovely piece." She reached out to touch one finger to the proudly arched little head, half-surprised to feel cool glass beneath her touch, rather than the warmth of a living creature.

"It's hard to believe that a human being could create something so exquisite," he murmured, talking to himself as much as to her.

"It's nice to be reminded of the good things we're capable of."

"Yes."

He looked past the Pegasus, his eyes meeting hers. Charity felt her color rise, and she hoped he'd attribute it to the warmth of the sun that poured in the front windows. She could suddenly hear Diane's voice suggesting that she should ask him out to lunch. It was so loud in her mind, she would hardly have been surprised if he heard it, too.

Watching the color come into her cheeks, Gabe wondered at its cause. She was really a very attractive woman, he thought, not for the first time. If he were honest, he would have to admit that it was her smile that kept him coming back to this particular store. He could have gotten the little crystal figures at a better price elsewhere.

Twice he'd almost asked her out. Each time he'd changed his mind. She wore no rings, but he couldn't believe that a woman with a smile like that wasn't seriously involved with someone. Besides, what if she accepted his invitation and then turned out to have the personality of an angry pit bull once she was away from her job?

Gabe rather liked having her in the back of his mind as a gentle fantasy. He wasn't sure he wanted to risk spoiling it with reality. God knows he had plenty of reality in his job.

But seeing her standing there with the sun picking out gold highlights in her honey-colored hair, with those big green eyes smiling at him, Gabe decided it was worth taking a chance.

He opened his mouth to ask if she'd consider having dinner with him sometime. The sharp ping of his beeper interrupted him before he could say anything. Grimacing, he set the Pegasus on the counter and reached for the beeper at his belt, silencing the electronic demand.

"Is there a phone here that I could use?"

"In the employees' lounge," Charity said. "Well, it's only a little room, really. But there's a phone there."

It was strictly against the rules, of course. Mr. Hoffman would frown severely if he found out she'd allowed a customer into the inner sanctum. But this was hardly an ordinary customer, Charity told herself, as she led the way to the back of the store. Not only was Gabriel London a regular patron, he was a police officer of some sort. She'd seen the badge several times when he took out his wallet to pay for his purchases.

Sally was just leaving the small room that went by the rather grandiose title of employees' lounge when

Charity led Gabe down the little hallway. There were boxes stacked in one corner, revealing its true use as a storeroom. But there was a narrow sofa crammed against the wall next to a table that held a coffee machine, a couple of magazines and the phone.

Sally gave Charity a surprised look as she showed Gabe into the room. He murmured his thanks and moved toward the phone. Charity wasn't surprised to find Sally waiting for her at the end of the narrow hallway.

"Hoffman'll be furious," Sally said, not without a certain amount of satisfaction. She resented the fact that though Charity didn't have the title, she had the authority that went with being a manager. If anyone should be unofficial manager, Sally felt it should be she. After all, she'd been with Hoffman's six months longer than Charity. Never mind that she couldn't manage her own checkbook, it was seniority that should count.

"Mr. Hoffman certainly wouldn't object to my lending a hand to a police officer," Charity said calmly.

"Who say's he's a cop?" Sally's tone was ripe with suspicion.

"I do." The calm statement was difficult to argue with, though Sally looked as if she'd like to give it a try. Luckily for Charity's patience, the soft ping of the bell over the door announced the arrival of a customer. The subject was dropped as both women moved toward the front of the store.

Sally took the first customers, an older couple looking for a gift for their granddaughter's graduation. Hard on their heels was a couple in their thirties who headed straight for the engagement rings. Charity wondered if everyone in the world but her was married or about to be. With a small sigh she moved toward them.

She'd just set a tray of rings on the counter when the bell pinged again. Glancing at Sally, she saw that she was still showing her customers a delicate diamond tennis bracelet. Unless Al bothered to come out of his office, the new customers were simply going to have to wait.

Charity looked at the new arrivals and felt her heart give a sudden, sickening bump. Three men had entered, all of them in their early to mid-twenties. Two were unshaven, their faces covered with a ragged growth of beard. A good bath and a delousing would go a long way toward improving their social standing.

They didn't look as if they were interested in buying an anniversary gift for their ailing mother, she thought, and then chided herself for being so judgmental. They were probably perfectly nice young men. Right. And pigs really could fly.

Charity murmured an apology to her customers and moved toward the newcomers. Stopping at the end of the counter, her hand dropped casually behind it, her fingers hovering over the silent alarm button. It might not be fair to judge them by their looks, but if that trio was here for anything but trouble, she'd eat her shoes, which couldn't possibly be more uncomfortable than wearing them.

"May I help you?"

The inquiry seemed to amuse them. They glanced at each other, mouths curving in smiles that did nothing to reassure Charity.

"Can you help us?" That was the clean-shaven one, the one with the pale blue eyes.

"Yes. Is there something I can do for you?" Charity kept her smile firmly in place, despite the shiver that was working its way up her spine.

"Well now, that all depends," he said mockingly. "It all depends on whether you got what we want." He turned toward her as he spoke and Charity felt her uneasiness crystalize into fear. Despite the warmth of the late-spring day outside, they were all wearing jackets. As he turned toward her, his jacket swung away from his body, giving her a clear look at the rather large gun tucked in his belt.

"What is it you're interested in?" she asked calmly. Her smile frozen in place, Charity's finger came down on the silent alarm. The signal would be relayed directly to the police department. And if she was misjudging these men and they were really undercover cops, she'd apologize later.

"Well, we're interested in a lot of things." The clean-shaven one must be the leader. He took a step toward her, a truly sickening smile on his thin face. But he didn't get a chance to continue.

Al Kocek, for whom quick wit could not be placed high on his list of attributes, chose this particular moment to demonstrate why that was the case. The silent alarm had triggered a red light and a discreet buzzer in his office. Charity speculated later that he'd probably been sleeping on the sofa when the alarm startled him awake. There were any number of intelligent reactions he could have had. Unfortunately he bypassed all of them.

"Who the hell triggered that alarm?" His bellow preceded him as he charged from the back hallway.

Everything seemed to happen in slow motion. The man who'd been approaching Charity spun around, his hand reaching inside his coat. When it came back out, the gun was clutched in his fist. She reached out, thinking to push him off balance, but he wasn't close enough. Her fingers barely brushed the sleeve of his coat. The gun lifted and she saw his finger tighten on the trigger.

The sound of the shot was deafening. Charity threw her hands up to cover her ears, turning her head to see Al Kocek's bulky body jerk with the impact of the bullet. Red bloomed on his shoulder. He staggered and fell back.

There was a moment of unbearable silence. It was broken by a scream. For a moment Charity thought the screaming in her mind had become audible. But then she saw Sally's mouth open, her eyes bulging with terror as she stared at Al's motionless body. She dropped her hands from her ears, not surprised to find them shaking.

Sally's scream broke off into loud sobs that filled the shocked silence.

ON THE PHONE at the back of the jewelry store, Gabe listened as Annie gave him a rundown of a report that had just come in. They'd been investigating an extortion racket for nearly three months and it looked as if they might finally be getting a break.

"Okay, I'll be there in a few minutes and we can go over it," he said. "Good thing I didn't have a hot date tonight."

It was probably just as well he hadn't had a chance to ask the saleswoman out, he thought ruefully. If she'd accepted and then he'd had to cancel, it would hardly get their relationship off to a good start. He'd ask her to hold the Pegasus for him. He could come in next week, strike up a conversation and then suggest dinner.

"You mean you'd prefer a hot date to an evening with me, sugar?" Annie's question pulled his thought back to the present.

"It's a tough choice, but duty calls."

"I think it'll be..." Gabe lost the thread of her words, his head jerking toward the open doorway as a large man ran by, his shoulder bouncing off the doorjamb. The contact didn't slow him.

"Who the hell triggered that alarm?" His angry demand came back to Gabe. The words were answered by the sharp, unmistakable crack of a .38.

Instinctively Gabe dropped to the floor, his right hand reaching for the gun tucked in the back of his waistband.

"Report a 211 in progress at Hoffman's Jewelry on Maple." His staccato words cut Annie off in midsentence. He heard her suck in a quick, startled breath before he continued in a low voice. "There's been a shot fired. I don't know if anyone's been hurt. We could have a hostage situation."

"Where are you, Gabe?" Her voice was all business, the slow Southern drawl gone.

"In the back. I'm going to try and get a look at what's happening."

"You be careful." Personal concern for him crept through her professional tone. "And don't do anything stupid."

"Believe me, I've never felt smarter." He set the phone down and eased to his feet, gliding over to the doorway.

The shot had been followed by a moment of shocked silence, and then a woman started screaming. From where he was, he could see nothing of the front of the store, which was both good and bad. He couldn't see what was happening, but they couldn't know he was here.

"Shut up, bitch!" The barked order cut the wailing off in midshriek. Gabe dropped to his knees and tried to remember the layout of the store. The hallway was off to one side of the main building, which meant that, unless someone was standing at the back of the store, in direct line with the hall, they wouldn't be able to see anyone in the hall.

Drawing a quick breath, he eased his head around the door, half expecting to have it shot off. There was no one in sight. But if anyone came down the hall, he'd be a sitting duck, probably a dead one at that. A gun and a badge were unlikely to endear him to whoever had fired that shot. They might have already killed one person. Shooting a cop wasn't likely to bother them.

He drew back into the employees' lounge, his eyes scanning it for anything that might be of help. There was nothing. In the distance he could hear the wail of sirens, which meant Annie had relayed the information that shots had been fired. Probably his presence, as well. So here came the cavalry. Great, as long as their arrival didn't precipitate a slaughter.

He hesitated and then jammed his gun back into the holster. Lifting one foot, he struggled with his boots, pulling off one and then the other. Stuffing them behind a box, he shrugged out of his jacket and tucked it in with them. He sincerely hoped he would be back to get them.

In his stocking feet, he padded back to the door. Once again he eased his head around the doorway. The hall was still clear. Reaching back to pull out his gun, he slipped into the hallway. In a half crouch, he moved silently down the hallway, ducking behind one of the jewelry cases at the back of the store.

He still couldn't see anything, but the low murmur of voices became clearly audible. As he listened intently, he formed a mental picture of what was happening.

"Look what you did!" The voice was young and nervous. "We weren't goin' to shoot anybody."

"The guy came barrelin' outta there like a freight train. What was I supposed to do? Ask him to tea?" This voice was older, a little guttural.

"Shut up, both of you." There was a certain crispness to the third voice, a tone that said he expected to be obeyed. Gabe immediately pegged him as the leader.

"But, Sal, look what Joe did." That was the young one, whiny and scared.

"Shut up!"

Outside, the sirens had screamed to a halt in front and in back of the store. Gabe already knew the back door was useless. A desk and a couple of office chairs crowded the narrow hallway in front of it. Maybe they'd just redone the office and hadn't had a chance to get rid of the old furniture yet. Maybe the owner was just careless. Whatever the reason, the back door was effectively blocked.

In a crouch Gabe crept forward, halting at the end of the case, unwilling to risk crossing the gap between it and the next case. He could hear car doors slam outside. There was a vague murmur that told him the stores on either side of Hoffman's were being evacuated, the employees and customers taken out the back doors, herded into the safety of the parking lot.

"Sal, there's cops all over the place." That was the nervous one again. Gabe marked him in his mind. Nervous people with guns were one of his least favorite things. If someone was going to go off half-cocked and start trouble, it was likely to be the nervous one. Or, obviously, the one who'd already shot the guy who'd come barreling out of the back room.

"That man is bleeding. He needs medical attention." The calm feminine tone was like a drink of cool water. Gabe recognized the voice of the little clerk with the big green eyes, sounding just as cool as if she were asking whether they'd like to pay by check or credit card.

"Let him bleed." That was Joe, the one who'd fired the shot. "Sonofabitch shouldn't'a come out shouting like that."

"I'd like to put a pressure pad on his wound," she said, ignoring the comment. Gabe didn't doubt that she was addressing Sal. "If he dies, it will be murder."

There was a moment's frozen silence while the three would-be robbers absorbed this piece of information. Gabe's fingers tightened on the gun. She was taking a risk, pushing like that. The nervous one and the guy who'd fired the shot both sounded tense.

"See what you can do for him," Sal ordered roughly.

They all seemed to be at the front of the store. Gabe's fingers tightened around the gun as he eased forward until he could look through the gap between the two cases. The wounded man lay directly in front of him. Blood had stained the front of his jacket. Probably not as bad as it looked, Gabe thought. There wasn't enough blood for the bullet to have hit an artery—didn't look as if he was in any danger of bleeding to death.

He slid back out of sight as the girl came into view. What was her name? Chastity? No, but it was something with an old-fashioned ring to it. Charity. That was it. Charity.

Why hadn't he asked her out before this? It would have been nice to have a better feel for how she was going to react in this situation. She seemed calm so far.

He heard the soft scuff of her shoes on the carpet as she approached the wounded man. Leaning his head back against the case, he debated his next move. She had probably forgotten that he was here. Was it smart to remind her? On the other hand, it might be helpful to have an ally.

Drawing a shallow breath, Gabe eased his head around the edge of the case...and looked directly into Charity's wide green eyes. She didn't look in the least surprised. She hadn't forgotten him for a minute.

"Anybody else in the back?" Sal's question was so perfectly timed, he might have been following a script.

Without so much as a flicker of an eyelash, Charity answered. "No. There's no one else in back."

"Check it out, Billy."

"Me? What if there's cops back there?" Billy asked nervously.

"If there were cops back there, we'd have been looking down the barrels of their shotguns by now," Sal said impatiently. "Just go make sure nobody else is hiding in the john."

Gabe knew that when Billy rounded the end of the last case, he had only to glance sideways to discover that there might not be cops in the back, but there was one right under his nose.

Holding his breath, he listened to the sound of Billy's footsteps, cursing the carpeting that muffled them. Praying that his timing was right, he swung into the gap between the cases just after Billy walked by it. Now he was visible only from the front.

Charity's eyes flickered up to him, her hands busy putting a pad against the oozing wound high in the unconscious man's shoulder. The lacy edge identified the makeshift bandage as a half slip.

Gabe heard Billy's boots strike the uncarpeted hallway. He could slip in behind him and eliminate at least one of the bad guys. But that would simply alert the other two to his presence and would do nothing for the remaining hostages. Just how many hostages were there?

As if she'd read his mind, Charity spoke. "You don't really need to hold all of us, you know. Why don't you let the two couples go? And Mr. Kocek needs a doctor. That would still leave you with Sally and me."

Someone—Sally, no doubt—uttered a squeaky protest. Gabe barely heard. Two couples, two employees and the wounded man. Seven hostages. More than enough to bargain with. Hearing Billy's return, he counted slowly to five before sliding back behind the case and out of sight.

Leaning his head back, he tried to decide what to do. He was right in the middle of a very nasty hostage situation with no way to communicate with the cops outside.

It was not a good situation, and he had a strong feeling that it was going to get worse.

Chapter Three

"How'd the cops get here so fast, anyway?" That was Billy, his voice stretched tight with nerves.

"Stay back from the windows, you idiot," Sal told him.

"Well, how'd they know?"

Billy moved away from the front windows, his movements quick and nervous. Charity found it difficult to take her eyes off the gun he was waving around so carelessly.

"That guy said something about a silent alarm," Joe said suddenly.

She swallowed hard and dropped her eyes to Al Kocek's still form.

"Who set off the alarm?" Billy demanded. "Couldn't'a been the old geezers, and the two of you don't work here, either." He dismissed the customers. His attention settled on Sally, who was cowering behind one of the cases, her heavily made up eyes bulging with terror. "You work here."

Charity had never in her life heard so much menace in anyone's voice. She could almost forgive Sally for her quick denial.

"It wasn't me. I wasn't anywhere near a button," she stammered out, her voice squeaky with fear. "It was her. Charity was right next to it. She must have set it off." One brightly lacquered nail pointed to where Charity knelt beside the wounded man.

Billy was beside her before she had a chance to do more than draw a quick breath. Grabbing her arm, he jerked her to her feet.

"Did you call the cops on us?"

The stubble of beard made him look younger, she thought, focusing her mind on that irrelevant detail. And a haircut would have gone a long way to improving his appearance. Where was Vidal Sassoon when you needed him?

"Did you push the damn button?" His fingers tightened on her arm. He gave her a rough shake. She'd have bruises tomorrow. Always supposing he didn't kill her today. "Answer me!"

"You had guns," she said finally.

"Bitch!" There was no time to avoid the blow, even if he hadn't been holding her. The back of his hand connected with her face, the force of it weighted by the gun he still held. Pain exploded through her face, radiating outward from her cheek until her whole head pounded. She would have fallen but for the hold he still had on her arm.

"You've ruined everything," he said shrilly, drawing his hand back to strike again. Over his shoulder Charity glimpsed a movement in the opening where she'd last seen Gabriel London, and her fear took on a new edge. If he moved to help her, it could set off a shoot-out that would leave all of them dead.

"Billy!" Sal's sharp voice stopped the blow. "Leave her alone."

"But she ruined everything," Billy whined. His hand dropped but he didn't release his hold on her arm.

"Hitting her isn't going to change anything. Come here. The cops are going to be calling any minute. We've got to figure out what to do next."

Billy released her arm reluctantly, a quick slashing look telling her that he wasn't going to forget just who had set off the alarm.

Charity had to lock her knees to keep from sinking to the floor. Her pulse was pounding in her ears, throbbing in rhythm with the pain in her bruised face. She could taste the salt tang of blood from her split lip. She didn't need anyone to tell her that she'd just come close to death.

Seeing their captors huddled together working out a strategy, she dared a quick glance to the side. Gabe's eyes were on her puffy cheek, and she could sense his frustration. She wanted to give him a smile, reassure him that she was all right. But her face was too stiff to allow such a movement.

The shrill ring of the phone was startling in the tense quiet. Everyone's eyes locked on the instrument, which sat on one of the cases. Sally must have made a call and left it out, Charity thought absently. Normally the phone was out of sight. It rang again, a sharp demand for attention.

"You figure that's the cops?" Joe asked.

Sal nodded. "Bound to be. They'll want to know what we want."

"You think if we ask 'em to go away, they'll do it?" Billy giggled like a nervous schoolboy. Sal ignored him. The phone rang a third time.

"Answer the phone. You." He gestured to Charity.

"What do you want me to tell them?" she asked over the fourth ring.

"Just answer the damn phone," Joe snarled. It was obvious that the tension was getting to him.

"I'll tell you what to say once you've got them on the line," Sal told her.

Charity nodded and walked stiffly to the phone. Apparently she was about to get a crash course in hostage mediation.

GABE LEANED his shoulder against the case. Sweat trickled down his spine, though the room was not overly warm. His left thigh was starting to cramp, he'd been so still so long, and he shifted position, moving gingerly, aware that a sound could cost him his life. He rubbed at the tight muscle until it relaxed.

How long had it been? A glance at his watch confirmed that it was only five minutes later than the last time he'd looked. Not quite an hour since this situation had begun. It felt like days.

The negotiations weren't going well. In fact they were hardly going at all. He didn't have to be outside with them to know that the police were as frustrated as he was. Sal's first demand for a helicopter had been nixed when the negotiator pointed out that there was no place to land it. When he'd asked for a van, the negotiator had demanded the release of a hostage. Gabe guessed that Sal might have gone for it, but Billy and Joe adamantly opposed letting even one of the hostages go.

The last call had ended in a stalemate almost twenty minutes ago. Charity had been doing all the talking, relaying the police demands to the three would-be thieves. Gabe's admiration for her had climbed steadily as the minutes ticked by. The pressure was incredible, but her voice remained level, without a hint of the fear she must be feeling.

From where he sat, the only hostage he could see was the wounded man, who hadn't regained consciousness. His chest continued to rise and fall, his breathing reasonably steady. The others he could only hear. There was an elderly couple. The wife had asked if she could open her purse to get her husband's nitroglycerin tablets. He guessed the other couple was younger, though all he could hear was an occasional low murmur of reassurance from one to the other.

That left only the other clerk, the one who'd been so quick to inform Sal and company just who had pushed the alarm button. Gabe had a vague image of her—a brassy redhead with a rather pouty expression.

He got occasional glimpses of Charity when she came to check on the wounded man. Their eyes would meet, but she was careful to look away quickly, afraid to draw attention to his presence. Gabe's gaze lingered on the dark bruise beginning to show on her cheekbone, and his fingers tightened on the gun.

There was no reproach in her eyes, no questioning why he hadn't done anything to protect her. She knew as well as he did that the only thing he could have done was get himself killed. But that knowledge didn't stop the guilt from gnawing at Gabe's stomach. He was a police officer. His job was to defend and protect. So far he'd done precious little of either.

"Why don't they call back?" That was Billy, his voice higher and tighter than it had been the last time he spoke. "Why the hell don't they call back?"

"Chill out. They're playing a waiting game with us, that's all," Sal said.

"Well, I don't like it." Joe's voice held a ragged edge that made Gabe uneasy. Billy might sound hysterical but Joe was the one who'd shot the man who lay on the floor. "I think they're bringing in reinforcements. That's what I think."

"Maybe I don't care what you think," Sal said. For the first time, his voice was taking on an edge.

Gabe felt the adrenaline start to pump. The tension was getting to all of them. Tense people with large guns and little to lose—a potentially deadly combination. The sharp ring of the phone made him jump. From the vivid curse, he guessed he wasn't the only one it had startled.

"Answer it," Sal snarled. Gabe eased forward between the two cases. He could see the edge of Charity's skirt, a soft flow of peach cotton. She picked up the phone, cutting it off in mid-ring. Gabe listened as she relayed the conversation.

The police were willing to provide them with a van but they had to release the hostages first. Sal's reply was short and pithy—they all went together or they could take the hostages out in body bags. The negotiator suggested that a show of good faith would go a long way to resolving this situation.

And so it went, back and forth. The negotiator bargaining for time; the robbers bargaining for their freedom. The call went on, Charity's quiet voice relating the negotiator's words and repeating Sal's replies.

Gabe could feel the tension building. Something had to give soon. The hair on the back of his neck was standing on end. He had to make a conscious effort to ease his grip on the gun. In his mind he marked where the three men were, trying to hold a picture of the store layout, judging their position from the sound of their voices.

Please, God, let them hit on a compromise. The last thing they needed was for anyone to open fire in the relatively close confines of the store. Too much chance of innocent people getting shot. But something told him his prayers weren't going to be answered.

He was right.

"Screw the damned cops," Joe exploded suddenly. Gabe heard Charity's gasp and then the crash of the phone being slammed through one of the glass cases. "I can't take this no more. If they won't give us what we want, we'll just have to show them we mean business."

Gabe heard a shriek and he knew the time for waiting was over. Whatever thin thread had been holding the situation in some tattered order was broken now.

"Police. Drop your weapons." He lunged up from behind the cases, taking in the situation at a glance. One burly gunman had hold of an elderly man, a pistol pointed at his head. The other two were ranged behind him on either side of the store.

For an instant the scene was frozen, like a tableau on a stage. No one moved, no one seemed to breathe. Gabe held his weapon trained on the man holding the hostage, wondering if there was any hope that they'd simply lay down their guns as ordered. There wasn't.

"What the—" Joe, in a reckless moment, thrust the old man aside as he turned his gun toward Gabe. Gabe's bullet caught him in the throat, and the bullet that had been aimed at Gabe's head buried itself in the ceiling as Joe's finger tightened convulsively on the trigger.

Immediately two other bullets shattered the glass counter where he'd been standing. But he was moving even as he fired, throwing himself down and to the right, his shoulder hitting the carpet as he rolled, drawing the fire farther away from the hostages. Rolling to a half crouch he snapped off another shot, the .45 slug catching a thin young man in the chest. The impact threw him backward into the front window, which shattered under the impact.

Gabe turned, rising to his feet to get the third and last gunman in his sights. But he'd misjudged. The other man had moved, even as he had. There was nothing but air where he'd been. Gabe swung around, feeling something tug his sleeve as the boom of the shot reached his ears.

And there was the third man, his face twisted with rage, his gun pointed right at Gabe's heart. For a split second, they faced each other over their drawn weapons. There was a moment, hardly more than a heartbeat, when Gabe thought the man was going to see the futility of it all; when he thought it might end right there.

Then he caught a flurry of movement out the corner of his eye. A flash of brassy red hair as one of the hostages snapped under the strain. She darted forward, shrieking mindlessly. In the instant before she came between them, the robber fired. Gabe felt the bullet brush past, a hairbreadth from his head. He dropped to his knees in a diving roll, coming up against the edge of a display case. A bullet shattered it, showering him with shards of glass. A third plowed into the wood just in front of his face.

Shaking his head, deafened by the continuous roll of sound, Gabe brought up his gun. He felt it recoil in his hand just as he heard a sharp cry.

"Sally! No!"

With horror, Gabe saw Charity stumble in front of him as she attempted to knock the other woman out of the way. Her body jerked with the impact of the bullet—his bullet. She half turned, her hands flung out, and then she crumpled to the floor.

Chapter Four

"They said she was in surgery, Gabriel. I'm sure she's goin' to be just fine." Gabe caught Annie's worried glance as she turned into the hospital parking lot, but her words didn't ease the tension that knotted his gut. Annie hadn't been there. She hadn't seen Charity fall.

He'd sleepwalked through the preliminary report. He'd answered the questions, given all the details, but his thoughts had been elsewhere—in the ambulance with Charity, in the emergency room. The paramedics had told him nothing, and he hadn't delayed their departure with questions they couldn't answer.

As soon as the investigating officers released him, Gabe headed out the door. He didn't protest when Annie took his arm and steered him away from his old Jag toward her more sedate four-door.

"Gabriel, you've got to believe she's going to be all right." She let a trace of exasperation creep into her voice as she searched for a parking place.

"Danny Androte wasn't."

"This ain't the same thing at all," Annie said. "You were shootin' at Danny Androte. This woman just happened to stumble in the way. Chances are the bullet just grazed her. She'll be just fine and she'll have an interesting story to tell her grandchildren."

Gabe didn't respond. She hadn't been there. The bullet hadn't grazed Charity. As soon as the car came to a stop, he was out the door. Swearing softly, Annie yanked the keys out of the ignition and snatched up her purse. She had to trot to catch up with Gabe's long-legged stride. She grabbed hold of his arm, pulling him to a stop.

"You go storming in there, looking like that, and the nurses will have you tranquilized and in a bed before you know what hit you."

Gabe looked at her blankly, and she clucked her tongue in exasperation, gesturing to his torn and blood-spattered sleeve. He'd allowed the paramedics to cleanse and bandage the shallow wound, but he'd refused any other treatment.

"Here. Put on your jacket, at least. You should be in bed, resting, you know," she scolded. She helped him into the jacket that someone had thoughtfully rescued from the back room of the jewelry store. Gabe sucked in a sharp breath as he eased his bandaged arm into the sleeve.

"Comb your hair," Annie ordered briskly, handing him a comb. Gabe obeyed, taming the unruly locks by feel. "There now, you look almost human."

"Thanks, Annie." He handed the comb back to her, his eyes focusing on her for the first time since the shooting.

"I'm just doing my part to uphold the reputation of the police force," she told him briskly. "Anybody who saw you would think we were all untamed wild persons." Her precise use of the non-sex-specific term drew a half smile from Gabe but he was already moving toward the hospital again.

Gabe's nose twitched as they stepped into the lobby. What was it they cleaned hospitals with to give them that odd non-smell? It was, in its own subtle way, as powerful as a whiff of ammonia.

The nurse at the desk informed them that Ms. Williams was still in surgery. It seemed to Gabe that she gave him a disapproving look, as if she knew he was responsible for Ms. Williams's condition.

Annie followed him into the waiting room. There were two people already there: a tall blond man of imposing proportions and a stunningly beautiful woman. Gabe barely noticed them.

"I didn't even know her last name until the nurse gave it to me just now." He and Annie took chairs on the opposite side of the room from the other couple.

"I don't see as how that makes any difference," Annie told him briskly.

"No, I suppose it doesn't." Gabe stared at his hands where they lay on his knees. "Did I tell you how well she handled herself? She was so calm."

"You've got to stop talking like she was dead, Gabriel."

Gabe didn't hear her. "I was going to ask her out. She had the prettiest smile. Sweet."

"You can ask her out when all this is over."

"If I'd just been a split second faster." His hand clenched into a fist on his knee.

"You can't second-guess yourself," she told him firmly. "You did what you thought was right."

Gabe didn't respond. He knew she was trying to keep him from thinking the worst. She kept telling him that it was probably a minor wound. But he knew better. Annie hadn't been there, hadn't seen the impact of the bullet.

He closed his eyes but he couldn't shut out the images. They were locked in his head, replaying over and over again like a film loop. He'd gone over it time and again, trying to see what he should have done differently.

Had he reacted too quickly? Maybe misjudged the danger to the hostages? Should he have waited to see if Joe would calm down? But if he'd waited, the old man might be dead now. Could he have prevented the shoot-out by revealing himself earlier? Would the three of them have surrendered if they'd realized there was a cop on the premises?

"Stop it." Annie reached out and caught his hand in hers, squeezing it to make sure she had his attention. "You saved several lives today. Don't you forget that."

"What if she dies?" Gabe asked her, his eyes bleak.

"She's not going to die."

He wanted to believe that, but he kept seeing Charity lying there so still and quiet, the bright tint of blood staining the carpet beneath her.

Seeing the taut line of his jaw and knowing there was nothing she could say that would make him feel any better, Annie sighed and stopped trying. Right now the only thing she could do for Gabe was to be here for him.

She got up and moved over to the coffeepot that sat on a low table. Pouring two cups, her eyes met those of the exquisite blonde, reading the banked fear in those wide green eyes. Annie gave her a half smile, offering the sort of wordless sympathy one shares with strangers caught up in the same situation.

Carrying the coffee back to their seats, she pressed one cup into Gabe's hand. He stared at it for a moment as if uncertain of its purpose and then murmured his thanks before taking a swallow.

The problem was that Gabriel London was basically too damn sensitive to make a good cop. She studied him openly, knowing he was too absorbed in his thoughts to notice. There were those who took one look at his easy smile and the casual way he approached most things and labeled him a lightweight.

But Annie knew differently. In the years they'd been partners, she'd learned that there was no one more dependable than Gabe. And there was no one less deserving of the title of lightweight. In fact it was her considered opinion that he needed to lighten up a bit.

Being a police officer was never easy. There was a reason cops had such a high divorce rate; why so many of them had drinking problems. The stress was unbelievable. If you were smart, you found a release before it reached a critical level. Whether it was racquetball or going out into the woods every weekend and getting in touch with nature, you needed something to keep you sane.

And you had to learn to go easy on yourself; to accept that all you could do was your best. Annie couldn't think of anyone more tolerant of others' failings and less tolerant of his own. Gabe expected very little of those around him and an extraordinary amount from himself.

She finished the last of her coffee. If this woman didn't make it... She didn't want to think about what it would do to Gabe.

Gabe was aware of Annie's scrutiny, aware of her concern. He knew he should reassure her, tell her he was all right. But the truth was, he wasn't at all sure he was all right. If only Charity hadn't run between them. The other woman had been out of the way, in no danger. If Charity had just stayed where she was...

THE MINUTES ticked by, stretching into hours. Annie kept his coffee cup replenished and Gabe drank it, more to reassure her than because he wanted it. He forced himself to stop looking at his watch when he realized that less than a minute was going by between glances.

The couple across the room spoke occasionally, their voices an indistinguishable murmur. Most of the time Gabe forgot they were there.

As the hours inched by, even Annie ran out of optimistic words. The longer Charity was in surgery, the harder it was to believe her wound could be minor. Twice Gabe told Annie to go home. She ignored him, giving him a sharp look and telling him not to be a fool.

The hands on his watch had just crawled past midnight when someone at last came to the doorway of the waiting room.

"Are any of you here for Ms. Williams?" The man who spoke was short, middle-aged and paunchy. He wore surgical greens, his shoes still encased in cotton booties. He looked tired, but Gabe couldn't read anything beyond that in his eyes, no matter how desperately he tried.

Gabe jackknifed out of the chair, every muscle tensed. His fingers tightened over the paper cup he held, crushing it. He stepped forward, but before he could say anything, the tall blond man spoke.

"I'm Brian Williams, her brother. This is our sister, Diane."

The surgeon sent a quick glance toward Gabe but didn't question his obvious interest. "I'm Dr. Lang."

"How is she?" Diane bypassed the polite introductions, asking the question on all of their minds.

"We're cautiously optimistic about your sister's condition," the surgeon told her, not in the least offended by her abruptness.

"What does that mean?" Gabe asked.

Brian and Diane Williams looked at him, surprised. All the hours they had shared the waiting room, it had never occurred to any of them that they might be waiting for the same news.

"Her condition is stable at this point."

"But?" Brian pounced on the unspoken qualifier in Dr. Lang's voice.

"There is a bullet fragment lodged very near the spine."

Annie took the ruined cup out of Gabe's hand, closing her fingers over his forearm.

"Is she paralyzed?" Was that his voice? He sounded so calm.

"We don't see any reason to expect that," Dr. Lang said cautiously. "To tell the truth, Ms. Williams has been very lucky."

"Lucky?" Diane said incredulously.

"Considering the seriousness of her wound, yes, I'd have to say your sister was lucky. The fragment near the spine is certainly a cause for concern but it's not pressing on any nerves."

"Why didn't you remove the fragment?" Brian asked.

"There's less potential for damage if we leave it alone. Once her body has had a chance to heal, I don't think she'll even notice the fragment's presence, unless she has to explain it to an X-ray technician." His half smile went unanswered.

"But you can't guarantee that," Brian said, frowning.

Dr. Lang gave him a weary smile. "Mr. Williams, medicine is not an exact science. I can tell you, based on the experiences of myself and my colleagues, it is our opinion that your sister will make a full recovery. But only time will tell for sure."

"Can we see her?" Diane asked.

"If you want to wait an hour, then perhaps for five minutes. She won't be awake, of course. But you can sit with her."

"Thank you."

"I certainly hope those thanks are deserved," Dr. Lang said, with a smile that said he was confident they were.

The waiting room was completely still after he left. For a few moments it was all anyone could do to just breathe and feel some of the tension seep away. Of course, Charity wasn't out of the woods yet, but there was reason to hope, reason to believe everything was going to be all right.

"Excuse me."

Annie's hand dropped from his arm as Gabe turned toward Charity's brother. Now that he knew who they were, he could see their resemblance to their sister.

"I don't mean to sound nosy," Brian continued with a half smile. "But who are you?"

He heard Annie catch her breath as if to caution him. But Gabe was beyond trying to think of a clever response. He said the only thing he could think of.

"I'm the man who shot her."

The stark answer wiped the cautious friendliness from Brian Williams's expression. He'd been prepared to share his relief with a friend of Charity's. He wasn't prepared to find himself face to face with the man whose bullet had put her in the hospital. His reaction was instinctive.

Gabe didn't try to avoid the punch. In his own mind he deserved that and more. Brian's fist connected with his chin with jarring force. Gabe staggered back and would have fallen if Annie hadn't grabbed his arm.

It was doubtful that Brian would have thrown another punch. The first had been more a result of tension and worry than anything else. But if he had been inclined to more violence, he didn't have a chance. With a shocked exclamation, Diane grabbed hold of his arm. Annie released Gabe, stepping in between the two men, her expression stern.

"Maybe y'all don't realize that if it weren't for my partner here, your sister and a lot of other people would be dead." In the heat of emotion, her accent thickened, making her sound more like a southern belle than a police officer.

"The police explained to us what happened," Diane said, her finger still clenched around her brother's arm. "We know it was an accident." But she avoided Gabe's eyes. Like her brother she was obviously having difficulty getting past the fact that he was the one who'd shot Charity.

Without a word Gabe turned and left. Their accusing gazes were more than his bruised soul could take. Annie gave the pair a last glance that combined sympathy and annoyance before hurrying after her partner. Catching up with him at the elevators, she threw a quick glance at his face but said nothing.

She grabbed his arm as they left the hospital, steering him in the direction of her car. Gabe followed without protest, though he'd just as soon have walked off into the night alone.

Thank God Annie didn't regard conversation as a cure-all. He leaned his head back against the seat and closed his eyes, wishing he could shut out the events of the past twenty-four hours as easily as he could shut out the freeway.

He didn't open his eyes again until he felt the car slow down for an off ramp. Opening his eyes, he realized she hadn't driven him to the station to get his car or to his own home in Pasadena. Instead they were in Glendale, heading for the house Annie shared with her husband.

"I'm really not up for company tonight, Annie." It was an effort to speak. All he wanted was to be alone.

"I'm not takin' you home, Gabriel. You'll just sit there and brood, playin' it over and over in your head, wonderin' what you should have done different."

Since that was exactly what he'd had in mind, Gabe didn't even attempt to deny it.

"Maybe that's what I need to do," he said shortly.

"I ain't havin' it. Next thing you know, you'll be throwin' your badge off some freeway bridge like a character in a Clint Eastwood movie."

Since he'd also considered doing something along those lines, Gabe was reduced to silence. The problem with Annie was that she knew him too damned well.

"Look, I'm not going to be very good company." He made one last effort to dissuade her as she pulled into her driveway.

"Well, and here I was expectin' you to teach me to polka," she said with heavy sarcasm. "You aren't stayin' alone tonight, Gabriel. What a body needs at a time like this is good friends and a medicinal drink or two."

"Going to get me drunk?" He asked, half-smiling in spite of himself.

"It wouldn't hurt."

"Anyone ever tell you you're a pushy broad?" he asked as he pushed open the car door.

"All the time, sugar. All the time."

He followed her up the walkway to the comfortable home she shared with her husband, resigning himself to the fact that Annie was going to have her way. Maybe she was right. Maybe being alone wasn't the best idea tonight. But he doubted anything would make him forget what had happened.

No matter how many good friends were around, or how many shots of whiskey Annie managed to pour down him, nothing could blot out the memory of those seconds when he'd seen the bullet—his bullet— hit Charity. And then the bright, accusing tint of blood spilling onto her dress.

It was going to take more than company and alcohol to make him forget that.

Chapter Five

The hospital smelled just the same. That odd non-smell that was somehow more antiseptic than a whiff of pure ammonia.

Gabe's fingers tightened over the bouquet of flowers. Now that he was here, he wondered if he was crazy to have come. The last person Charity would want to see was him. He was the reason she was here.

He was determined to apologize—an empty gesture but it had to be made. Maybe he shouldn't have brought flowers. Maybe they were too frivolous. He frowned down at the bouquet of yellow roses. He'd stripped his neighbor's rose bush earlier this morning, wanting the kind of roses that had scent, rather than the hothouse sorts the florist carried. Jay would probably throttle him when he saw the denuded plant but he could worry about that later.

He stepped out of the elevator, pausing to ask directions to Ms. Williams's room. It was really a delaying tactic. He knew where her room was from his last two visits. But those times he'd talked himself out of actually seeing her. This time he intended to go through with it. The least he owed her was an apology and a chance to tell him how much she hated him.

Over a week since the shooting and still no sign of the feeling in her legs. The doctors insisted there was no reason to despair. The spine was a delicate area. It needed time to heal.

Gabe's steps dragged as he walked down the hall to Charity's room. He didn't want to see those big green eyes look at him with cold anger. Didn't want to hear her vent the rage she surely felt toward him. But he owed her that much.

He stopped outside her door, his hand so tight around the tissue-wrapped stems that his fingers ached. Like as not, she was going to throw his flowers back in his face and him out on his butt. Drawing in a deep breath, he knocked on the half-open door.

"Come in." Her voice was just as he remembered it. Soft, with a touch of huskiness. Gabe felt his palms break out in cold sweat. He'd rather have faced a drugged-out junkie with an AK-47 than walk through that door.

Taking a deep breath, he squared his shoulders and pushed open the door. Charity was propped up in bed, a pale pink bed jacket over her shoulders, her honey-blond hair pulled back with a matching ribbon. She was paler than he remembered, her skin almost translucent. She looked so fragile, so young.

Gabe stopped just inside the room, waiting to see the smile in her eyes change to hatred when she realized who he was.

"Mr. London." The smile reached her mouth, her lips curving. "Come in."

Gabe moved forward, walking carefully, as if the ground might shift under his feet at any moment, which was exactly how he felt. Didn't she remember what had happened?

"Hello." He stopped beside the bed. He was unable to sustain her gaze, and his eyes dropped to the roses.

"Those are beautiful," Charity said after a minute, when he showed no signs of speaking.

"They're for you." He thrust them out.

Charity took them, bent to breathe in the rich scent. "They're wonderful." When she lifted her head she was still smiling. Gabe didn't respond, only stared at her, as if he wasn't sure what he was doing here. "Would you mind putting them in water for me," she asked. "You could put them in that vase there. I think those flowers have about had it."

Gabe took the roses back from her mechanically. There was a mixed bouquet on the table next to the bed. The flowers were beginning to show their age. He dumped them into the trash and filled the vase in the little bathroom. Bringing it back into the room, he set it on the table and put the roses into it.

"They look perfect. And the scent is wonderful." She turned her head to smile at him. "Thank you, Mr. London."

"Call me Gabe," he said automatically. Shooting someone should surely put them on first-name terms, he thought, wondering if he was dreaming this visit.

Obviously she didn't remember what had happened, didn't realize that he was the one who'd shot her. He felt a wave of relief. He didn't have to see the friendliness turn to hatred, didn't have to hear her tell him that he'd destroyed her life.

"I'm the one who shot you," he said abruptly.

"I know."

Nothing changed in her eyes. She was still smiling at him. Gabe groped for something to hold on to, finally grabbing the rail at the foot of the bed.

"Don't you hate me?"

"No. Why should I?" She seemed genuinely puzzled.

"Why should you? Because it's my fault you're here. *I shot you,*" he said again, in case she hadn't heard.

"But you didn't mean to."

"That's not the point."

"It was an accident," she said, handing him the same words he'd been hearing from Annie and the police psychologist ever since the shooting. "It wasn't your fault. If it was anyone's fault, it was mine for running in front of you like an idiot."

"You were trying to save the other woman's life," Gabe said, stunned to find himself defending her to herself.

"Well, as it turned out, she wasn't the one in the way." Charity shrugged. "It was just bad timing all around."

"And that's it? You don't want to tell me you hate me? You don't want to throw something at me? Yell and scream?"

"I don't think so. Would it make you feel better if I did?" Charity smiled at him mischievously, relieved when his mouth relaxed in a rueful smile.

"I don't know. I was so sure you'd be angry. That you'd hate me. I'm not sure I know what to say. Thank you, I guess."

"You don't have to thank me."

"I wouldn't have blamed you if you'd hated me."

"Well, I don't. If it wasn't for you, that poor old man would have been killed and probably a lot of others, including me. Besides, it's not as if I'm paralyzed for life," she said, hoping he couldn't hear the brittle note in her cheerful words.

"What do the doctors say?" She could hear the strain in his voice.

"Oh, you know how doctors are." Charity shrugged. Her eyes skittered over the length of her legs visible beneath the blankets, fixing on his face instead. Seeing the worry in his eyes, she forced a smile. "They tell me there's no reason why I won't walk again. It's just some bruising, I guess. As soon as it's healed, I'll be tap dancing.''

The fear in her eyes brought a sharp pain to Gabe's chest. The fact that she was trying to hide it only made it more heartbreaking. He'd have given his right hand if doing so would have given her back her legs.

"Did you tap dance before?" he asked, forcing a light tone, even as his fingers tightened over the rail at the foot of the bed, the knuckles white with strain.

"No." Charity grinned at him, the expression less forced. "But when I asked the doctor if I'd be able to, he assured me I would."

"Did you tell him you hadn't been able to before?"

"No. I was all set to do my best Groucho and say 'That's funny. I couldn't before.'" Her Groucho voice was moderately dreadful but Gabe couldn't suppress a grin.

"Why didn't you?"

"He looked so serious." She sighed regretfully. "I just didn't have the heart to tell him I'd been joking."

"Probably would have done him some good to lighten up a bit," Gabe suggested.

"Probably, but I figured as long as I was stuck in this place, it wouldn't be a good idea to annoy the staff. They might do something really hideous, like bring me more than three meals a day."

"Food's that bad, huh?"

"Worse than bad." Charity shuddered, seeing the smile on his mouth slowly creep into his eyes. "It's so bland, it's deadly. After a few days of this stuff, I'd just about kill for a pizza."

Gabe's smile became a chuckle. Charity relaxed back against the pillows, taking pleasure in seeing some of the tension ease from his features.

When he'd first walked in, he'd looked like a man on his way to a firing squad. White lines of tension had bracketed his mouth and his eyes had held a look of despair that had made her heart go out to him. Now he was beginning to look like the man she remembered, the one with the easy smile that had lingered in her thoughts more than it should have.

It was odd that the nervousness she'd always felt when he came into the store seemed to have faded. What they'd gone through together had created a connection between them that left no room for nerves.

In those terrible, tense hours of waiting, listening to each attempt at negotiation fail, wondering if she was about to die, Charity had held fast to the knowledge that Gabe was there. It didn't matter that their only contact was a brief meeting of their eyes when she checked the wounded man's bandage. It didn't matter that there was little he could do. Just knowing he was there had given her something to cling to when she felt her self-control slipping away.

She'd known even then that it wasn't Gabe's badge that convinced her everything would be all right. It

was Gabe himself. There was a quiet strength about
him that had reassured her.

"Mr. Kocek, the man who was shot first, is going to
be all right."

"I heard. That's good."

Charity's eyes searched his face, seeing the lines of
strain that hadn't been there before the shooting, the
tightness around his mouth. He didn't look as if he'd
done much smiling lately.

"They told me that the others—the two you..." The
words trailed off as she groped for the right words.

"The ones I shot?" Gabe finished for her. "They
died."

"Yes." She wished she hadn't said anything. The
look in his eyes was painful to see.

"Yeah, I was batting a thousand that day."

She saw his knuckles whiten where he gripped the
low rail at the foot of her bed. She looked away,
smoothing her hand over the covers beside her as if it
was important to remove every wrinkle.

"You know, if you hadn't...done what you did, a
lot more people would have died."

"Maybe." Gabe shrugged. "It's a little hard to feel
good when two men are lying in the morgue and
you're here, like this." He gestured to her legs.

"You did the right thing," she said, her soft voice
firm. "You didn't see them the way I did. They would
have shot that poor old man. And it wouldn't have
stopped there."

"That's what I tell myself." Gabe's mouth twisted ruefully. "Sometimes I almost believe it."

"You should believe it all the time."

Gabe only shrugged again, but the lines that bracketed his mouth were less deep, his eyes a little less bleak. Inside he was marveling at her generosity of spirit. She was lying in a hospital bed—where he'd put her—without the use of her legs, and yet she was concerned that he not feel guilty.

She should have hated him. Instead, she was trying to make him feel better. It didn't ease his gut-deep guilt. Nothing could. But he felt his interest in her deepen.

They talked, more easily than either of them would have expected. Gabe had spent some time in the hospital when he had his appendix removed, and they compared notes, coming to the conclusion that hospitals had their good points but the food definitely wasn't one of them. Neither could explain why the nurses woke you to take a sleeping pill.

Gabe's description of the lengths to which he'd gone to try and get a full night's sleep made Charity laugh, something she hadn't done much of the past few days.

He didn't stay long. Charity murmured a protest when he said it was time he left. In between bouts of sleep, the days had been longer than she would have thought possible.

"I don't want to tire you," he said.

"I'm not tired." But a yawn punctuated the sentence. Seeing Gabe's smile, she grimaced. "All I do is sleep," she muttered crossly.

"Probably the best thing for you."

"Now you sound like my doctor. You don't have a medical degree tucked in your pocket, do you?"

"You've guessed my secret." His smile faded, his eyes searching her face. "I'd like to come again, if you wouldn't mind."

"Are you kidding? I've considered begging strangers in the hall to come and talk to me. My brother and sister come in every evening but that still leaves a lot of hours to be filled."

"What about your parents?"

"Mom and Dad are off somewhere in the African bush doing whatever one does in the African bush. They don't even know I'm in here. Which is just as well. Mom would want to dose me with some of her foul-tasting herbs and Dad would be cross-examining the doctors."

"They sound great." It wasn't hard to read through her complaints to the very real affection she felt for her parents.

"They are," she admitted, wishing suddenly that Seth and Josie Williams would walk into the room. They'd be driving her crazy inside of an hour, but there was a certain comfort in their eccentricities.

She yawned again and Gabe stood up. This time she didn't protest when he said he had to leave. No doubt he had better things to do than entertain her.

"Thank you for the flowers."

"Thank my neighbor. I stripped his rose bushes before coming over here." Gabe shrugged. "He's probably waiting for me with a shotgun. I'll have to bribe him by promising to help him haul in a load of manure next spring."

"You can assure him that they were greatly appreciated," Charity told him, reaching out to touch one soft blossom.

"That'll console him." He hesitated, pushing his hands in the pockets of his jeans, his smile fading. "Are you sure it's all right if I come again?"

"Yes. But don't feel you have to. What happened was an accident. You weren't to blame. Besides, it isn't as if I'm stuck this way for life," she added with a forced smile.

Charity was torn between relief and regret when Gabe left. Regret because she didn't really expect to see him again. And relief because she didn't have to keep the happy face in place anymore—at least not until Diane and Brian came to visit in a few hours.

She watched the door close behind Gabe and closed her eyes against the sudden hot sting of tears. Tears she was determined wouldn't fall. She hadn't cried since waking up after surgery—not when they'd told her she'd been shot, and not when it had become obvious that she had no feeling in her legs.

Crying would be an admission that she was frightened. And if she was frightened, it would be an admission that she might never walk again. As long as she kept telling herself and everyone else that her paralysis was a temporary setback, she could keep from going completely crazy.

But sometimes, when she was alone, it was hard to keep the doubts at bay. There was nothing to keep her from staring at the lifeless lengths of her legs, wondering if she'd ever be able to feel them again.

Opening her eyes, Charity blinked to clear the tears from her vision. It was only natural that she'd have moments of doubt, she told herself. The important thing was to make sure that they didn't last. A positive mental attitude was vitally important to her recovery—that's what everyone said. If she heard it again, she was going to scream.

Put one of the doctors or nurses with their cheerful smiles in this bed and take all the feeling from their legs and see how long they kept a positive mental attitude. No, that wasn't fair. They were just trying to help.

She sighed, turning her head to look at the roses Gabe had brought her. Their rich scent was already filling the room, making the air less sterile. She reached out and eased one fat blossom from the vase, lifting it to her nose.

She wondered if he'd meant it when he said he'd visit again. Probably not, but it had been nice of him to say it. The rose held against her cheek, she let her eyelids drift shut.

IN FACT Gabe showed up the next day. Charity had been staring at the television mounted near the ceiling opposite her bed. But her interest in game shows was slight, to put it mildly. Diane had brought her a stack of books, but she could only read so many hours in the day. She was discovering that one of the worst things about being in the hospital was the boredom.

A small movement near the door drew her attention. She knew she had to be going over the edge when even the thought of a technician taking another blood sample was a welcome diversion. But it wasn't a technician, and she felt her heart skip a beat when she saw Gabe's lean frame.

"Is the coast clear?" he hissed before she had a chance to say anything. *Clear for what?* She nodded and he disappeared back out the door. Her curiosity piqued, she dragged herself higher against the pillows, for once hardly noticing that her legs were unresponsive.

When he ducked back through the door, he was carrying a box. The flat white shape was unmistakable even if the rich scent of oregano and tomato hadn't already told her what he was carrying.

"Pizza!"

"Shh. If they catch me, there's no telling what they'll do to me. They might even make us share." He pushed the door shut with his foot. He set the box down on the rolling table at the foot of the bed and lifted the lid.

"You brought pizza." Charity's lowered voice was reverential.

Gabe grinned, pleased with her reaction. He'd had his doubts about the advisability of visiting her again. She'd said he was welcome but he hadn't quite believed her. He couldn't help but think that every time she saw him, it must be a reminder of what had happened. But there'd been nothing but welcome in her eyes.

"Pizza with the works, just like the lady ordered," he said. He reached into the sack he'd brought, coming up with two plates and a handful of napkins.

"It smells heavenly."

He lifted out a thick slice dripping with cheese and set it on a plate, which he handed to her with a flourish.

Charity picked the pizza up and bit into it, closing her eyes in ecstasy as the rich taste filled her mouth. Her tongue came out to catch a bit of sauce on her upper lip and Gabe was startled by a sudden flash of awareness.

He dropped his eyes, not wanting her to see what might be written there. He set a slice of pizza on a plate for himself, though he wasn't particularly hungry.

Careful, London, he cautioned himself. The attraction he'd felt for Charity had to be put aside—one of those sweet, foolish dreams that wasn't meant to be. She might welcome his presence now when any distraction was welcome, but there'd come a time when he was only a reminder of a painful and frightening episode in her life. If that time came when she was walking again, he'd bow out of her life without regrets.

He suppressed the doubting voice that suggested that the regrets were likely to be fierce and hard to shake off.

"Something wrong with your pizza?" Charity's question brought Gabe's head up to meet her quizzical expression.

"I always consider the first bite very carefully," he told her condescendingly. "There's an art to these things."

"Of course there is," she agreed. "And the most important aspect is how fast you can eat. Otherwise, someone else gets more. Another slice, please, garçon." Grinning, she handed him her empty plate.

Gabe pushed away the uneasiness he felt and settled down to a serious competition. At the moment the most important thing was to see her smiling.

"I CAN'T BELIEVE that guy had the nerve to visit you!" Brian Williams scowled at his youngest sister, who returned the look calmly. It was a source of unending wonderment to her that this certified genius who was revolutionizing the computer industry had a temper more suited to a guard dog.

There was none of the stereotypical computer nerd about Brian. No glasses, no hump-shouldered posture from too many hours at a keyboard, no ink stains on his shirt pocket. He actually looked more like an athlete, which he was, than a computer whiz.

"I don't see any reason why Gabe shouldn't visit," Charity said calmly.

"No reason?" Brian's blue eyes expressed his amazement. "Would you explain it to her?" he appealed to Diane and then gave Charity the explanation before Diane could say anything. "The man shot you. It's his fault you're in here. His fault you can't walk."

"Temporarily," Charity corrected, her voice tight. "Temporarily can't walk."

Brian paused, realizing how tactless his words had been. "Of course it's temporary," he said gruffly. "But that's not the point."

"No it isn't," Charity agreed. "Even if the paralysis were permanent, it still wouldn't be Gabe's fault. You weren't there, Brian. You don't know what the situation was. He risked his life to keep those men from shooting any of the hostages."

"Yeah, right. So they didn't shoot them. He did," Brian said with heavy sarcasm.

"It was an accident. I've told you that before. I'm the one who got in the way. If I'd stayed where I was, this wouldn't have happened."

"You were trying to save that woman's life," Brian said, leaping to her defense.

"And he was trying to save all our lives." She lifted her hand when he would have continued. "I don't want to hear any more about it, Brian. I know you're worried about me and I appreciate it, but I like Gabe and if he wants to visit, he's welcome."

Brian shut his mouth with an audible snap, glaring at her. Charity returned the look calmly. After a moment he looked away, muttering something about stubborn women and people who didn't know what was good for them.

"I'm going to get a cup of that stuff they call coffee," he announced abruptly. Charity watched him leave the room and turned to look at Diane.

"Don't start," she warned. "There's nothing wrong with Gabe coming to see me."

"Of course not, Char." But Diane's beautiful eyes showed her concern. "We just don't want to see you hurt. After all, Mom and Dad aren't here and we're the only family you've got."

"If you're trying to tell me that Mom and Dad wouldn't approve of Gabe, I don't buy it. Mom would have baked him some of her inedible whole-wheat oatmeal surprise cookies and Dad would want to know his opinion of teaching Latin in high school.''

"Probably," Diane admitted, smiling reluctantly. The truth was, their parents had never met anyone they didn't approve of. They could have found something good in Jack the Ripper.

"It *wasn't* Gabe's fault," Charity said for what felt like the hundredth time.

"I know. I really do," she emphasized, catching Charity's disbelieving look. "I just worry that...well, you've got to admit you're sort of vulnerable right now." She spoke slowly, choosing her words with care. "I don't want to see you hurt, Charity. Neither does Brian."

"You think I might be reading too much into Gabe's visits?" Unconsciously Charity reached for the teddy bear Gabe had brought only that afternoon, saying he'd thought the bear looked like it needed some company. She kneaded her fingers in the soft, dark fur.

"This is the guy you mentioned the day before...before this happened." Diane's graceful gesture encompassed Charity's useless legs. "When we were having tea and I was bugging you about not dating. You said there was a man you found attractive. I remember the name, Gabriel London."

Charity frowned, trying to remember the conversation. That quiet afternoon seemed a hundred years ago. Yes, she remembered mentioning Gabe, but it had been just in passing. He'd popped into her head for some reason when Diane was urging her to date more.

"Just because I mentioned him, said he was attractive, doesn't mean I'm stupid enough to think the man is in love with me," Charity protested. "I know he's only visiting because he feels guilty."

"I'm sure he likes you," Diane protested.

"Sure he does. That's my problem, remember? Men always *like* me." Charity rolled her eyes to show that it didn't bother her a bit. "The only reason he isn't telling me about his girlfriend is because he feels sorry for me."

"Does he have a girlfriend?" Diane asked, and Charity knew she was hoping he did. If Gabe was already involved, there'd be less chance of her getting hurt.

"I'm sure he does." She shrugged, ignoring the small ache the idea brought to her heart. "A man like Gabe isn't likely to be running loose." She plucked restlessly at one stuffed ear, wishing Diane would stop looking at her with that worried expression.

She wasn't a child who still believed in fairy tales. She knew perfectly well that once she was walking again, Gabriel London would walk right out of her life. But in the meantime, there was nothing wrong with enjoying his company. He made her laugh. These days, that counted for quite a lot.

It wasn't as if she were going to do something stupid ... like fall in love with him.

"YOU CAN'T GO back to your apartment, Char. Be reasonable."

Gabe paused outside Charity's room. In the week he'd been visiting, he hadn't run into her sister or her brother, but it looked as if that was about to change.

"I don't see why not," Charity said, and Gabe wondered if it was his imagination that put an audible strain in her voice.

"How about the fact that there's a flight of stairs leading up to it? You can't manage those in a ... in a wheelchair." Diane stumbled over the word.

Gabe winced at the mental image of Charity in a wheelchair. His hands clenched into fists in the pockets of his light jacket. There was still no feeling in her legs. The doctor claimed that it was just a matter of time. Her body had taken a tremendous shock, it needed time to heal. She couldn't be impatient.

Easy to say if you weren't the one facing a wheelchair, Gabe thought fiercely. It wasn't right that Charity should suffer like this. It was his mistake, his misjudgment that had put her there. If he'd just shot a split second sooner or later ...

"Since I don't plan on going anywhere, I don't see that it matters." Gabe dragged his attention back to the conversation on which he was eavesdropping.

"You can't just shut yourself up in that apartment," Diane protested.

"Well, I'm not likely to be taking any long trips anytime soon," Charity pointed out, her voice beginning to sound a little ragged around the edges.

It was the sound of that stress that brought Gabe into the room. He'd gotten to know her in the past few days. He'd admired her determined cheerfulness even while he wondered what it cost her to smile when she must be screaming with fear and anger inside. He couldn't stand to hear the strain in her voice that said she was close to losing that control.

"Hi. Not interrupting, am I?" Both women turned to look at him as he pushed open the door. The brother wasn't there, he saw at a glance. A man the size of Brian Williams would be a little hard to overlook.

"Gabe." Charity's smile told him she was grateful for the interruption. "I thought you said you wouldn't be able to get in today."

"Well, there was a break I hadn't expected so I thought I'd drop by."

"I'm glad you did. I don't think you know my sister, Diane. Diane, this is Gabriel London."

"Actually, we've met," Gabe said, his eyes meeting Diane's and seeing the uneasiness there.

"You did?" Charity glanced at her sister, surprised that Diane hadn't mentioned meeting Gabe. "When?"

"The night you were brought in," Diane said. "Gabe was in the waiting room. With a friend of his," she added. "A very pretty woman."

Gabe wasn't sure just what the glance she threw Charity was meant to convey, but he didn't want Charity to get the wrong idea about Annie.

"My partner," he said easily. "She and her husband are friends of mine, as well." That should clear up any lingering impression that Annie was more than a friend, he thought. Though why it should seem important, he couldn't have said.

"Oh." The flat syllable could have meant anything, but Gabe had the feeling Diane Williams didn't like hearing that Annie was nothing but a friend, and a married one at that. He could ponder the reasons she might feel that way later.

"I thought I heard you talking about going home," he said to Charity. "Are they releasing you?"

"In a couple of days. There's really no reason for me to stay in the hospital. It's just a matter of waiting now. I can do the physical therapy as an out patient."

"Are you going back to your apartment?"

"She can't. There's about a thousand stairs leading up to her apartment. Maybe you can make her see reason," Diane said, willing to apply to any port in a storm.

"I'm not coming to stay with you," Charity told her, irritated. "The carpets in that apartment are about six inches thick. If I have to learn to use a damned wheelchair, I'm not going to do it on those carpets.''

"I'll tear the stupid things up.''

"I'm sure your landlord would love that. Besides, quite frankly, a week of living with you and we'd be at each other's throats. I love you dearly, Diane, but you are not my idea of a great roommate.''

"I have a cleaning service,'' Diane said huffily.

"No cleaning service in the world could keep up with you.'' Charity reached out and caught her older sister's hand. "I really do appreciate the offer, but I need peace and quiet right now and those are not things I associate with you.''

Diane looked as if she wanted to argue but couldn't. "Well, fine then. Don't stay with me. But you'll go back to your apartment and shut yourself in like a hermit over my dead body.''

"I don't want to be a hermit,'' Charity said. "But it's the most practical arrangement. When Brian gets back from Europe, he can help me get upstairs and then he can take me to physical therapy a couple of times a week. He might as well use those muscles for something besides lifting barbells.''

"I don't like it,'' Diane said sullenly.

"I don't, either.'' It was obvious that they'd forgotten Gabe's presence, from the surprised expressions they turned on him.

"Don't you start,'' Charity wailed in exasperation.

He shrugged. "Sorry. But I don't think it's a good idea. An apartment whose access is only by stairs is dangerous. What if there was a fire?"

"Exactly," Diane said in triumph, glad to have an argument Charity couldn't dismiss.

"Do you have a better idea," Charity asked sarcastically.

"Actually I do. You can move in with me."

Chapter Six

"What?" Charity and Diane spoke simultaneously, giving the word a stereo effect.

"Move in with me," Gabe repeated. "It's the perfect solution."

"I don't see how," Diane said, obviously removing him from her list of allies.

"That's because you haven't seen my place," Gabe said without rancor.

"Gabe, it's awfully nice of you to offer but you don't have to—"

"I know I don't have to," he interrupted. "I want to."

"But—"

"Before you start making objections, let me explain why it would be so ideal."

Charity subsided but her expression remained doubtful. Diane didn't even bother to look that positive. Gabe felt like an insurance salesman pitching a policy to a resistant client.

"I've got a house in Pasadena—a good neighborhood. It's one story, all hardwood floors. There're three bedrooms and two baths so we wouldn't get in each other's way."

"It sounds lovely but I don't—"

"There's also a pool out back that you could use for physical therapy. You wouldn't have to come to the hospital all the time, and my next door neighbor is a doctor," he added as a final incentive.

Diane's expression had gone from total rejection to interest. He could see that she liked the idea of having a doctor next door. Charity didn't look any more convinced than she had when he started.

"It's really nice of you, Gabe," she said. "But there's no reason for you to disarrange your life. My apartment isn't as bad as Diane makes it sound. And if it really won't do, then I can find someplace else."

"Why find someplace else when my place is so close to ideal?"

His hands braced on the foot of her bed, he leaned forward. It was important to him to get her to agree to this. She might *say* that it wasn't his fault that she still couldn't walk, but he would never believe it. He'd fired the shot that had put her in this hospital bed. There was a fragment of his bullet still inside her.

If he could help her, even in so small a way as giving her a place to stay, it might make it a little easier for him to sleep at night.

"You know, Charity, he could be right," Diane said thoughtfully. Charity gave her sister a surprised look. Wasn't it Diane who'd urged her to be careful about getting involved with Gabe? Seeing Charity's expression, Diane shrugged defensively.

"Well, it seems like a reasonable solution. There's no stairs to worry about and the pool would mean you could probably do more physical therapy than if you had to come into the hospital for it every time."

"I could stay with Brian," Charity suggested desperately, feeling as if a gentle trap was closing around her.

"Brian's place isn't big enough to swing a cat," Diane reminded her. "Besides, his hours are far from normal. He's as likely to be working at three in the morning as he is to be sleeping."

"I don't want to be in your way," Charity said, giving Gabe a pleading look.

"You wouldn't be," he assured her, knowing it wasn't what she wanted to hear. If she stayed with him, he could keep an eye on her, make sure she had everything she needed. Maybe in some small way, he could make up for putting her in here.

Charity looked from Gabe to Diane, seeing her fate already decided in their eyes. Staring down at the outline of her lifeless legs, she wanted to scream and pound her fists against the unresponsive flesh, demand that the feeling come back so that she didn't have to depend on other people.

She wanted to insist on going back to her apartment, her nice, safe little apartment where everything would be familiar and normal. Only nothing was going to be normal until she could walk again. If she went back to her apartment, Gabe and Diane were both going to worry about her—Brian, too, when he came home. They'd feel obligated to check on her, to make sure she had everything she needed.

She sighed. Realistically she knew they were right. Walling herself up in her apartment wasn't going to make everything right again. And staying with Gabe would give him a chance to ease some of the guilt he shouldn't be feeling in the first place.

"If you're absolutely sure I wouldn't be in your way," she said slowly, lifting her eyes to meet Gabe's. His smile made her heart beat just a little faster than it should, a reminder that this move had some inherent dangers. She was going to have to be careful that while she was regaining the use of her legs she didn't lose her heart.

"I DON'T KNOW, sugar. You sure this is a good idea?" Annie frowned at Gabe.

"It's a great idea. I've got plenty of room and she needs a place to stay. What could be simpler?"

"You don't think maybe you're carrying this whole guilt thing a bit too far?" she asked, settling into her favorite perch on the corner of his desk.

"She can't walk because of me, Annie."

"Now, don't go getting your dander up, Gabriel." She lifted a soothing hand.

Gabe closed his eyes for a moment and drew a deep breath, forcing the tension out of his shoulders. There was no reason to snap at Annie. She was just concerned about him.

He opened his eyes and gave her an apologetic smile. "Sorry."

"That's okay. What good are friends if you can't snap at them now and then?"

"That's an interesting view of friendship," he said, stretching his legs out and crossing them at the ankles.

There were any number of reports sitting on his desk awaiting his attention. In twenty minutes they were supposed to observe a lineup, and in an hour they had to go convince a store owner to testify against a suspect they'd arrested.

At the moment the only thing Gabe could think of was the fact that he was picking Charity up at the hospital this afternoon and taking her back to his house. He'd done everything he could think of to prepare the place for her to manage from the wheelchair.

"What time do you pick her up?" Annie asked, as if she'd read his thoughts.

"Five. I borrowed Levowitz's van so there'd be room to get the wheelchair in with no problem. Her sister will be coming back with us, too. I'm going to have to do something about a car," he said, frowning. "The Jag isn't going to cut it."

Annie gave him a sharp look. "Not that I wouldn't love to see you get rid of that old heap of junk," she said carefully. "But don't you think getting a new car is carrying this whole thing a bit far? The shooting was an accident, Gabriel. You wouldn't be human if you didn't feel bad about what happened, but don't go rearranging your whole life."

"Charity's whole life has been rearranged," he said shortly, wishing she'd quit looking at him like he needed a few more sessions with the police psychiatrist.

"I'm not denyin' that. But you can't make her well, Gabriel. And puttin' bars up in your house and ramps on the steps and gettin' rid of your car ain't goin' to make her walk. Only time'll help that."

"I know that," he said impatiently. "Look, everybody is busy telling me that it's not my fault she can't walk and maybe you're all right. But it *feels* like it was my fault, and if I can help her by giving her a place to stay while she gets well, I don't see anything wrong with that."

"Of course not. If it'll make you stop beatin' yourself up, then I'm all for it. I just don't want to see you get hurt."

"I'm not going to," he said grumpily, tired of having his motives questioned. He was simply helping a friend. There was nothing all that complex about it.

CHARITY SMOOTHED her fingers nervously over the skirt of her dress, checking that it was lying smooth over her knees. Diane had brought the dress to the hospital yesterday. The full skirt draped over her legs, falling almost to her ankles when she was seated, which of course was the only position she was in lately, she thought painfully.

She'd thought she was anxious to leave the hospital, until the time actually came to get dressed and pack. Then she'd suddenly realized how safe and secure she felt there. No one stared at her when the nurses wheeled her down the halls because chances were they were in a wheelchair, too. No one stared and wondered what was wrong with her. They had their own problems to deal with.

But once she left the hospital, she wouldn't be normal anymore. She'd be in the real world where people who walked were normal and people in wheelchairs were something less.

It took all her willpower not to beg the doctor to let her stay, just another day or two. If she willed it hard enough, surely she could get the feeling back in her legs. He was wrong in thinking she was ready to leave. She wasn't ready at all. She wanted to stay here where she was safe and insulated.

As long as she was in the hospital, her paralysis was a temporary thing. Once she left, she'd be forced to start learning to manage in the real world. And every new skill she picked up, every problem she conquered, would be another sign that she wasn't ever going to walk again. It was as if learning to cope without the use of her legs would cut her off from ever using them again.

But there was no way she could explain her confused fears to anyone else. And even if she could make them understand, she couldn't expect them to keep her in the hospital just because she was afraid to leave.

So she'd struggled into the dress, trying not to look at her legs even when she had to lift them to put them in place. She hated touching them, hated feeling the lifelessness of them. That was something else she hadn't told anyone.

No matter how hard she tried, she couldn't make the connection between these unresponsive limbs and *her* legs. *Her* legs moved. She could feel blood pumping through them and hot and cold air against them. She could feel the swish of a skirt or the scrape of shrub brushing against them.

Now, sitting in her room, waiting for Diane, she smoothed her skirt again, unable to feel the pressure of her hand against her knee. If it hadn't been for the fact that she could see her legs, could touch them, she wouldn't have known they were there.

She looked away from them, fighting back tears. She had to believe that she was going to walk again. If she didn't believe that, then she would surely go crazy. The only thing that kept her sane was the thought that this whole thing was just a temporary nightmare. Soon the world would be back to normal. She'd be able to go on with her life again.

She heard Diane's voice greeting one of the nurses and forced the fears into the back of her mind, tilting her mouth up in a smile that didn't reach her eyes. If she could just keep pretending everything was going to be all right, then surely it would be.

Perhaps Diane sensed her nervousness or maybe she was uncertain about this move herself. She kept up a cheerful patter all the way to the lobby, talking to the nurse who was pushing Charity's wheelchair when Charity's responses were slow in coming.

Charity could feel her stomach starting to churn as the elevator door slid open and she was wheeled out into the lobby. The light seemed much too bright and there were far too many people. She knotted her hands together on the arms of the wheelchair, fighting the urge to beg the nurse to take her back to her room.

They stopped at the lobby desk where one of the volunteers cut the plastic I.D. band from her wrist, making a small ceremony out of it. The woman probably thought she was going to get up out of the wheelchair as soon as she was wheeled outside, Charity thought. She had no way of knowing that for her, leaving the hospital was more frightening than staying.

Stop feeling sorry for yourself, she ordered herself sternly. *It could certainly be worse.*

At the moment that was cold comfort indeed.

The doors whisked open with an electric whoosh and Charity was outside for the first time in two weeks. The air was hot and dry, tightening the skin on her cheeks, harsh to lungs accustomed to the air-conditioned atmosphere of the hospital. She squinted against the sun that poured over the pavement beyond the sheltered area in front of the hospital.

A slightly scruffy blue van pulled up in front of them, blocking her view of the circular drive. The driver's door slammed and then Gabe was walking around the front of the vehicle, his long stride filling Charity with a sense of her own inadequacy.

She looked up at Diane, her hand reaching up to clutch her sister's sleeve, ready to go back into the safety of the hospital, anything to keep from having to face a normal, *walking* world.

"Madam, your chariot awaits." Gabe stopped in front of her and swept a theatrical bow, one hand extended toward her, a pure white rose held in his long fingers.

"Oh." Charity's hand trembled slightly as she reached to take it from him. "It's beautiful," she said softly, raising it to her face.

"Its beauty pales before thine," he told her, pressing one hand to his heart and giving her such a soulful look that laughter dried the tears trembling on her lashes.

She felt better suddenly. Looking into his eyes, the fear receded. Somehow it was hard to be afraid when Gabe was there.

"Thank you, Gabe."

"De nada," he said, shrugging as he straightened. "I raided Jay's prize rose bushes again."

"Won't he be upset?" Charity knew that Jay Baldwin was the doctor who lived next door to Gabe and a good friend as well as neighbor.

"Not if no one tells him who did it," Gabe said, with a smile.

"My lips are sealed," she assured him.

The nurse wheeled her over the curb where the van waited. Gabe pulled open the door, and Charity stared at the step as if it were a viper. How many times had she stepped in or out of cars in her lifetime and never given it a thought?

But Gabe didn't give her a chance to dwell on the fact that she couldn't take the step for herself.

"Allow me." Bending, he scooped her out of the wheelchair and into his arms as if she weighed next to nothing.

Startled, Charity's wide eyes met his, only inches away. She couldn't feel the arm under her legs, of course, but she could feel the one across her back, hard and strong, as if he could hold her forever.

Even more startling than the easy strength with which he held her was the sudden awareness she felt, a tingle that started in the pit of her stomach and worked its way up to catch in her throat.

For a moment Gabe's arms tightened around her, his eyes more gold than green, and she wondered if he felt the same shiver of awareness. His eyes dropped to her mouth and she felt the impact of that glance as if it was a kiss. Her breath caught, her heart beating too quickly.

The sound of a car horn in the street broke the fragile tension. Gabe blinked, his hands shifting as he turned toward the van. An instant later he'd set her on the seat. Charity felt a real sense of loss when he drew away.

She shook her head. It wouldn't do to start imagining things. She had enough problems without adding a pathetic crush on Gabriel London to them. This was exactly what Diane had warned her about, and she'd dismissed the warnings. Now she knew she had to be on her guard. It shouldn't be hard to remember just why Gabe was so concerned. All she had to do was look down at her legs to be reminded.

GABE HANDED CHARITY the end of the shoulder seat belt, smiling in response to her murmured thanks. He wondered what had put that sudden bleak look in her eyes. Not that she didn't have reason enough. But a moment before, when he'd been holding her in his arms, her eyes had been full of promise, deep green and warm, like a tropical sea.

He shook his head as he walked around the front of the van. The only thing he needed to be concerned about at this point was getting Charity home and getting her well. The fact that holding her had been like holding a piece of heaven was not important right now.

No one had much to say during the drive to Gabe's house. Gabe pretended to concentrate on his driving. Charity stared out the window, pretending that nothing was wrong, that she'd be able to get out of the van without help. Seated in the back, Diane stared at the wheelchair folded into the space next to her, wishing she could just slide open the door and push it out onto the freeway, along with her sister's need for it.

The house was, just as Gabe had said, in a nice neighborhood, middle-class and tidy—the sort of place where children played in the streets, moving out of the way of the van before reclaiming the best skateboarding surface around.

Gabe pulled into his drive and shut off the van. For the space of several seconds, no one said anything. It was as if they were all just realizing that this was really happening.

Charity's fingers knotted together in her lap. She couldn't do it. If she'd thought it was hard to leave the hospital, it was nothing compared to the thought of getting out of this van. Gabe would put her in the wheelchair and everyone would be able to see that she couldn't walk.

"We're here," Gabe announced in a tone of forced good cheer.

"It's very nice," Diane said.

Charity didn't add anything to the stilted conversation. Her chest felt tight, as if all the air was being cut off. She couldn't do this. They were all wrong to say that she was ready to leave the hospital. They had to take her back. Right this minute.

She looked at Gabe, ready to ask him to turn the van around, when the passenger door was pulled open.

"You all turned to statues or what?" Startled, Charity turned to look at the owner of the gravelly voice. Seated in the van, she looked slightly downward into a pair of deep brown eyes set in a square-jawed face. He wasn't handsome, not by any standard, but there was a sort of homely appeal in his features.

"I'm Jay Baldwin, Gabe's neighbor." He held out his hand and Charity took it automatically. "And the owner of the rose bush that came from," he added, gesturing to the rose that lay in her lap. He shot Gabe a threatening look. "I was thinking of calling the police to report the theft but I had a feeling they already knew."

"It was on my side of the fence," Gabe said virtuously.

"Funny, that bush is a good five feet from the fence."

"It sprawls," Gabe said.

"Ha. It would have to crawl to get that far."

Jay tugged open the back door, his eyes skimming over Diane's perfection with apparent indifference. "You must be the sister," he said, reaching for the wheelchair.

It was a new and not particularly welcome experience for Diane to hear herself described—and dismissed—as "the sister."

"Diane Williams," she said, but he only nodded as he lifted the chair out, unfolding it with a few practiced moves. It was obvious that he didn't care to pursue the acquaintance any further.

"You're not going to be able to maneuver in and out of a high seat like this on your own," Jay said, opening Charity's door. She unbuckled her seat belt in automatic obedience to his gesture and found herself unceremoniously lifted and set in the chair with a minimum of fuss.

There was no opportunity to say that she didn't need to worry about getting in and out of the van because she was going back to the safety of the hospital. No chance to feel self-conscious or awkward. One minute she was sitting in the van, the next she was being wheeled up the concrete walkway.

"Gabe's house is better for wheelchair access than most but you'll still have to learn how to handle this thing."

"I don't want to learn how to handle it," she snapped. They were the first words she'd spoken since Jay's arrival.

"Of course you don't." Jay shoved open the front door and pushed her into a wide entryway. "Nobody does, but you're luckier than most."

"Lucky?" At the moment she wasn't feeling particularly lucky.

"It's only temporary for you."

Charity felt a weight slip from her shoulders. Of course it was only temporary. She'd lost sight of that today. She'd begun to think she was always going to be in this chair.

She turned to grin up into Jay's square face. "Thank you."

"Don't mention it." He grinned down at her, the expression transforming his features from homely to roguishly attractive. Diane, walking in the front door, caught sight of him and stopped so abruptly that Gabe, following on her heels, bumped into her. Diane blinked, a slightly dazed look in her eyes as she moved out of the doorway.

For the next thirty minutes Gabe showed Charity around the house, familiarizing her with the layout as well as the changes he'd made to make it easier for her to manage on her own. Since she'd already rejected the idea of a live-in aide, he'd made a few strategic modifications.

Bars had been installed in the bathrooms, as well as a hanging bar over her bed so that she could pull herself up and get into the wheelchair without having to call for help. There was one step leading down into the living room and he'd installed a ramp over that so that there wasn't any room in the house where her wheelchair wouldn't go easily.

The only blight on the tour was the antipathy between Diane and Jay. When it came up that Diane had been a model, Jay's upper lip had shown a faint but definite tendency to curl.

"How interesting," he said with total insincerity. *Airhead,* his eyes said.

"I'm sure being a doctor is much more interesting," Diane snapped. *Prig,* her eyes flashed back.

From then on, any conversation that involved the two of them was more in the nature of a verbal boxing match.

Ordinarily Charity would have been intrigued by any man who didn't simply fall head over heels for her sister. That Jay Baldwin, who was not particularly tall, dark or handsome, showed no sign of succumbing to Diane's fatal charm would have amused her no end.

At the moment, nerves and the exhaustion of her first day out of the hospital were catching up with her. She'd never have believed how tired she could get after only a few hours out of bed, and all of them spent sitting down, at that. But tired she was, bone deep and muscle weary.

When Gabe noticed her pallor and suggested that she ought to get to bed, she didn't even bother to put up a token argument. Nor did she protest when Diane offered to help her into bed. She'd practiced getting in and out of the wheelchair at the hospital; remembering to set the brake, lifting first one leg and then the other off the footrests, then using her arms to pull herself into the bed. But tonight she wasn't sure she had the strength to make the switch from chair to bed.

Once she'd managed to convince Diane that she was really and truly settled in and didn't need her big sister to spend the night holding her hand, Charity was alone. She listened to the murmur of voices from the living room as Diane and Jay bade Gabe good-night. She felt more isolated and alone than she'd ever felt in her life.

Pressing the back of her arm over her eyes, she forced back the frightened tears. Crying never did anything but make her eyes red.

"Charity?" Gabe's voice was quiet as he tapped on the door. Sniffing, she wiped her eyes and dragged herself higher against the pillows before calling to him to come in.

"I just wanted to make sure you have everything you need." He stayed near the door, his hands pushed into the pockets of his jeans.

"Everything," she said and then winced at the forced cheerfulness in her voice.

"The bell there is in case you need me." He nodded to the decorative brass bell that stood on the nightstand.

"Oh. How thoughtful." She reached out to pick it up and the clapper pinged gently. She held it against her chest.

Gabe was relieved to see a genuine smile light her face. She looked so small lying there in her pink nightgown, her hair drawn back from her face. He'd had to push his hands in his pockets to keep from gathering her up in his arms and kissing the uncertainty from her eyes.

"I'm a light sleeper," he said when the silence threatened to stretch too long. "The least sound will wake me."

"That must make you uncomfortable to sleep with," Charity said without thinking. Hearing her words, she stared at him, eyes round, her fair skin flushing.

"I haven't had too many complaints," Gabe said slowly, his mouth curving in a suggestive grin.

"No, I don't suppose you have." And then she flushed even deeper. It had to be the shock of leaving the hospital that had addled her brain, she thought, wondering if this was a good time to fake amnesia and pretend to forget the past few minutes.

Gabe sensed her embarrassment and swallowed the comment he'd been about to make. If she got any redder, she was likely to explode. But she looked less waiflike than she had a few minutes ago.

"Well, I'll let you get to sleep," he said briskly. "Just remember to ring if you need me. Good night."

"Good night." Charity watched the door close behind him and waited for the loneliness to close in around her again. But it didn't. Rubbing her thumb lightly over the polished brass surface of the bell, she felt her mouth curve in a smile. She didn't feel alone anymore.

Chapter Seven

When Charity woke the next morning, for one bliss-ful moment she didn't remember where she was or why she was there. Sunlight poured in through the win-dow, spilling across the bed. From where she lay, she could see a slice of bright blue sky and a fluffy white cloud.

Maybe because for the first time since the robbery she was waking in a home, not a hospital room, her first urge was to get up and go to the window. She wanted to throw it open and draw in a deep breath of fresh air.

She threw back the covers, eager to do just that. And reality came crashing over her, shattering the sparkling mood, making the blue sky seem gray and overcast. Instead of sitting up and swinging her legs off the bed, she was stuck lying there like a bundle of old rags.

The disappointment was so acute, she felt tears burn her eyes. She forced them back and drew in a deep breath. Crying wasn't going to change things, she reminded herself briskly. The doctors said she just needed time to heal. If she kept up with her physical therapy and clung to that hope, she'd be walking again before she knew it.

Shoving the covers out of the way, Charity reached for the bar Gabe had hung over her bed and pulled herself into a sitting position. Glaring at the wheelchair, she began the rather arduous task of getting herself ready to face the day.

Well, there was one thing for sure, she thought an hour later, she certainly wasn't going to be making any impulsive trips anywhere. Just getting washed and dressed had taken more time than she'd ever dreamed.

Her back hurt with the strain of constantly stretching for things that were just out of reach. Her arms ached with the effort of compensating for all the things her legs would no longer do. Too bad she'd never learned to walk on her hands, she thought with a touch of black humor.

Now that she was dressed, she wasn't at all sure she wanted to leave the dubious sanctuary of her room. Gabe had told her that he was taking a couple of days' leave to make sure she got settled in. She appreciated his concern though she would have preferred some time alone to find out just how awkward she was going to be. But she could hardly have told him to stay away. After all, it was his house.

Charity eyed the plain wooden door like a track star eyeing the high hurdle. She could do this. After all, it wasn't as if Gabe hadn't already seen her in the wheelchair. She just had to go out and smile and show him that she was capable of managing on her own— she hoped—and he could go on about his own business. He probably had all sorts of things he wanted to do around the house.

BUT IT SEEMED that all Gabe had to do was watch over his house guest, which he did quite thoroughly. From the moment Charity pushed the wheelchair into the kitchen were he'd been drinking coffee, there wasn't a need he didn't anticipate.

He got a box of cereal from the cupboard for her, though it was on a shelf low enough for her to reach and he'd already told her that she was to make herself completely at home. He got the milk from the refrigerator before she had a chance to think of it. The sugar appeared as if by magic, as did a glass of juice and a slice of buttered toast, neither of which she particularly wanted.

When she was finished, he cleared the table. When she mentioned that she might go out on the patio, he opened the sliding door for her. Once outside, she drew a deep breath of fresh air, relieved to be alone. Until she happened to glance back at the house and saw Gabe sitting in a chair by the window, reading the paper in a place that just happened to put him where he could keep an eye on her.

Charity turned her head to hide a grin. She suspected he was going to drive her crazy, but there was something rather sweet about his concern.

GABE TRIED to concentrate on the paper but found his attention drifting to the patio. Was it warm enough for her to be out there, he wondered, frowning. Maybe she should have a wrap of some sort. The fact that the temperature was hovering in the mid-seventies and he was wearing running shorts and a T-shirt didn't register with him.

She was sitting awfully still. Was she in pain? Maybe trying to hide it? He'd already learned that Charity was quite adept at concealing what she was feeling. He hadn't known her long but circumstances had accelerated their acquaintance a bit.

She'd looked so frightened yesterday when he picked her up at the hospital. He'd taken one look at those wide green eyes and wanted to snatch her up and hold her close, promising that nothing would ever hurt her again.

He shifted uneasily, frowning at the newspaper he wasn't reading. He wondered if Annie was right—if maybe he was letting his feelings of guilt get twisted into something more dangerous.

The problem was that he *liked* Charity. The guilt was still there, gnawing in his gut every time he looked at her in that wheelchair. But it wasn't just guilt that had made him open his home. Nor was it guilt alone that made him want to put his arms around her and protect her.

He liked her. Worse, he was attracted to her. And it wasn't just those wide green eyes or the inviting fullness of her lower lip, though he had to be honest and say that those attributes didn't hurt. But there was more to it than that.

He liked the way her eyes could smile, even when her mouth didn't move. He liked the way she didn't have to fill every moment with conversation. He liked the way she nibbled her lower lip when she was thinking. In fact he liked just about everything he'd learned about her. He wished now that he had followed his impulse to ask her out months before this whole nightmare started.

Charity had wheeled the chair over to a rather scraggly planter box that sat on one corner of the patio and was nipping faded petunia blossoms from the plants. Somehow Gabe doubted that she was paying any more attention to what she was doing than he was to the paper he was supposedly reading.

A stray shaft of sunlight found its way through the louvered overhang and caught in her hair, turning it to pure gold. She looked rather like an angel he'd seen in a painting once, all soft and gentle. It was a wonder that a woman with so much to offer wasn't already involved with someone.

How do you know she isn't?

The paper crackled a protest as Gabe bundled it shut, his brows hooked in a frown. It had never occurred to him that Charity might be involved with someone, but there was no reason why she shouldn't be. The thought was not at all pleasant.

Of course, if there was someone in her life, surely he would have been to see her while she was in the hospital. He would have been consulted about her move into another man's house.

Unless the scum had deserted her when she didn't immediately regain the use of her legs. Maybe he'd been afraid she'd be permanently paralyzed, and he'd cut and run just when she needed him most.

Gabe's scowl grew fierce. Charity certainly deserved better than a guy like that. He was just contemplating the great pleasure it would give him to plant his fist squarely in the unknown boyfriend's face when it suddenly occurred to him that he didn't even know there *was* a boyfriend. He was furious with a man who might not even exist.

He shook his head and ran his fingers through his hair, rumpling it into even shaggier waves. God, this past couple of weeks must have taken a bigger toll than he'd thought. His imagination was getting out of hand.

He looked at Charity again, shooting to his feet when he saw her leaning forward, trying to turn on the outlet that fed water to a leaky length of hose. He all but sprinted through the kitchen and onto the patio. Didn't she realize she could fall?

"Here. Let me help with that."

Charity glanced up, startled by his sudden appearance. "I can get it."

"You shouldn't have to." Gabe took the hose from her and turned the outlet on with a quick twist. Water shot out the end of the hose as well as in delicate streams from several leaks along its length. "Where did you want it?"

"I just thought I'd put a little water on these petunias, if you don't mind. They looked a little dry."

"Probably extremely dry," he said, setting the end of the hose in the planter she'd indicated. "I'm afraid I'm not much of a gardener. Jay had some extra plants and he stuck them in here. I just don't remember to water them."

Looking at the desiccated soil, Charity thought that was self-evident. The Gobi Desert probably had a similar water content.

Gabe stood next to her, watching the water run into the planter. But she knew he was really waiting to see if she was going to do anything else that might require his assistance, like maybe blowing her nose.

He'd been hovering like a mother hen all morning. She appreciated his concern, really she did, but she wasn't *completely* helpless, and having him lurking over her shoulder was going to drive her crazy.

"Are you hungry or anything?" Gabe asked.

"I just ate," she reminded him, torn between the urge to laugh and the urge to hit him. Did he have to stand there looking so damned healthy? She felt frustrated and unattractive enough without him standing around looking so . . . so male.

"Yeah. Right." Gabe stared at the hose again. "You're not too cold or anything are you?" He gave her an anxious look.

"It's seventy-five degrees out here."

"Right. You're probably not cold."

"No, I'm not."

Silence while they both stared at the hose again. Charity waited.

"Are you thirsty? I could get you something to drink."

"No, thank you."

She'd thought that she had her voice under control, no hint of the fact that she was grinding her teeth allowed to show. But Gabe seemed to sense something. He shot her a quick look.

"Am I hovering?" he asked after a moment.

Charity considered saying no. She considered it for all of five seconds. But the thought of having him lurk over her every minute of the day brought thoughts of actual violence to mind. For his safety as well as her sanity, they had to come to some sort of understanding.

"Yes," she said, letting out the breath she'd been holding.

"Am I driving you crazy?"

"Yes." But she softened the affirmative with a smile. "It's not that I don't appreciate it," she added quickly. "I mean, it's nice that you're so concerned and all but..."

"But you're going to hit me if I don't go away," he finished for her, his mouth curving in a rueful smile.

"Well, not too hard."

He hooked one foot around a battered lawn chair and dragged it across the cement. Sitting down, he stretched his long legs out in front of him, meeting her eyes with an apologetic smile.

"Sorry."

"Don't be." Charity was relieved that he was taking it so well. After all, he'd been trying to be helpful. It seemed rather ungrateful of her to complain.

"I just want to be sure that you know I'm here in case you need anything."

"Believe me, I know you're here."

Gabe laughed. "That bad, huh?"

"No, not really. It's just that I'm a little self-conscious about... about this thing," she said, running her fingers over the arm of the wheelchair.

"You seem to be managing pretty well."

"Thanks." She sighed, wishing she could appreciate the compliment. She didn't want to manage the wheelchair pretty well. She wanted to be rid of the thing.

Staring out at the back lawn, still green from the winter's rains, she wanted to feel the grass under her bare feet. Hell, at the moment she'd settle for being able to feel her feet at all.

Maybe she sighed or perhaps Gabe read some of what she was feeling in her expression.

"You know, you don't have to pretend that everything is great all the time," he said quietly. "If you ever want to scream or throw things, don't feel you have to pull back because of me."

Charity's startled eyes met his. Sometimes it seemed as if he knew her; knew what she was thinking, better than he had any right to. For a moment she wanted to take him at his word, wanted to let some of her fears and frustrations out.

But she stifled the urge. She couldn't admit how frightened she was that the paralysis *wasn't* temporary, that she'd *never* walk again. She had to believe she was going to walk, had to believe that she was only trapped in the hateful chair for a short time. Admitting to fear would be admitting there was something to be afraid of. And there wasn't. This was all temporary. It had to be.

"I'm not really the screaming, throwing things type," she said lightly.

Gabe nodded, wondering if she was even aware of the way her hand was clenched into a fist on the arm of the chair. But he wasn't going to be the one to point it out to her. He knew what it was to cling to the ragged edge of control; to feel that if you let go, just for an instant, you'd somehow never find your way back to sanity again.

"I meant it when I said you were to consider this your home," he said.

"I know you did. I appreciate it." She also appreciated the change of topic. It would be all too easy to let go of her feelings of fear and anger, but she wasn't sure she'd be able to get them under control again if she ever once loosened her rigid hold on her emotions.

"Don't hesitate to change things around, if you need to," Gabe continued, watching the water run into the petunias.

"Well, I don't think I'm up for any heavy-duty furniture moving," she said dryly, hitting the chair lightly for emphasis.

"I can move furniture, if you want something changed."

"Thanks, but I don't think that will be necessary."

"And feel free to invite people over, friends or whatever," he said with a vague wave of his hand.

"That's generous of you, but I doubt if I'm going to feel much like entertaining." She rubbed the arms of the wheelchair absently.

"I just thought there might be someone you wanted to see." Gabe slanted her a sharp look and then returned his attention to the flowers. "I mean, someone special. A boyfriend, maybe."

The words were not quite a question, but Charity answered as if they were. "There's no one special."

Gabe felt a wave of relief. Strictly because he hadn't liked to think of her being deserted by someone she cared about, he told himself.

Charity stared at the redwood fence that surrounded the yard, wondering if what she'd said was entirely true. Could she really say there was no one special in her life? Her feelings for Gabriel London were perilously close to special.

What a disaster that would be; to fall in love with a man who felt, at best, friendship, and at worst, pity. Not that she was going to do anything that stupid. It was her legs that were paralyzed not her common sense.

CHARITY WAS AMAZED by how quickly life settled into a routine of sorts. It seemed that she was living proof of the endless human capacity to adapt.

Gabe stayed home for two more days, managing to resist the urge to hover. She was reluctant to admit it, even to herself, but Charity was glad to know he was there, just in case. Of course, she would have just about died rather than call on him for help, but it was nice to know that in an emergency there was someone there.

It surprised her to realize how quickly they'd established a certain routine. Gabe was up long before Charity made it out of the bedroom, and he had coffee brewing and breakfast made. He either ate breakfast with her or sat with her while she ate.

That half hour first thing in the morning was one of the few things she looked forward to. The more she knew Gabe, the more she liked him—his sense of humor, his ability to laugh at himself.

Most of all she liked their breakfasts together, because it was one of the rare occasions when she could almost feel normal. Sitting at the table made it possible to forget that she was sitting in a wheelchair; that she could not just get up and walk away at the end of the meal.

Moments like that were few and something to be treasured.

LIFE SETTLED into certain patterns. There was a comforting rhythm to the days. It was something to cling to when her mind began to drift to less pleasant thoughts, like the fact that her legs were still unresponsive.

Most of the time she managed to keep her spirits up. She tried to focus on how lucky she was to be alive at all. There were compensations. If it hadn't been for the shooting, she would never have gotten to know Gabe London as anything more than an attractive man who came into the jewelry store.

And while she might regret the circumstances, she couldn't regret her growing relationship with Gabe. On closer acquaintance, he was, if possible, even more attractive than when he was merely a customer. The charm that was so readily apparent was more than skin-deep.

He'd told her to treat his home as her own. It was more than a polite offer. From the moment she moved in, he acted as if the house was as much hers as it was his. Not once did he make her feel like an unwanted guest. It might have been a guilty conscience that drove him to offer her a place to stay, but you'd never know it. She was to make herself comfortable, he'd said.

But how could she feel comfortable in his home when she wasn't even comfortable in her own body? The question made Charity sigh. She'd been out of the hospital for a week now, and despite daily sessions with either the physical therapist or Diane, there was still no feeling in her legs.

Patience, everyone kept counseling. She had to give her body time to heal. In time she'd regain the feeling in her legs. She'd always considered herself an unusually patient person but she was finding it a difficult quality to hold on to.

Looking out the open window, she watched Gabe pushing an old-fashioned reel mower across the lawn. The soft clickety-clack of the reels and the rich scent of freshly cut grass filled the air.

Charity blinked back tears. She could go out on the patio where she could really savor the scent. If she wanted, she knew Gabe would wheel the chair out onto the grass for her or carry her out and set her on the sweet green lawn.

But she didn't want to be settled onto the grass like an infant. She wanted to run across it, feel it cool and soft beneath her bare feet. She wanted to roll on it; dance on it; revel in the feel of it. Instead she was trapped in this damned chair.

She knotted her hand into a fist, pounding it lightly against the arm of the wheelchair. Anger was good, the therapist had told her. Anger and frustration could be turned into determination. Despair was something else entirely, though. Despair was self-defeating, the first stage of giving up.

Easy for the therapist to say, Charity thought irritably, turning away from the window. She had two perfectly good legs. What did she know of how it felt to look at your legs and wonder if you were ever going to stand on them again.

"Stop feeling sorry for yourself," she whispered, trying to banish the dark mood. "You'll walk again. It's just a matter of time."

She thrust her fingers through her honey-colored hair, massaging the ache that had settled into the back of her neck. Most of the time she managed to keep a positive attitude; to believe everything was going to be all right. She'd smiled and looked cheerful until her face ached.

Everyone seemed to accept her good cheer at face value. Except maybe Gabe. Sometimes she caught him looking at her with something in his eyes that made her wonder if he saw through to the fear she was trying so hard to keep at bay.

She suspected that Gabe saw a great deal more than most people. That lazy smile and those never-quite-serious eyes made it easy to think of him as a lightweight. But you couldn't live with someone without getting to know them and the Gabriel London she was coming to know was a man of deep feeling.

A man who stirred her emotions far more deeply than was wise. Charity rubbed her fingers absently along the arm of the wheelchair. She was beginning to fear that while she was regaining the use of her legs, she was losing her heart.

Chapter Eight

The house was early-morning quiet. Outside, the sun had barely crept over the horizon and the birds were just starting to wake up, sending out an occasional sleepy chirp to test the day.

Charity guided her wheelchair noiselessly down the hall. She breathed a little easier once she'd turned into the living room. Making her way across the smooth expanse of hardwood floor, she eased over the threshold that divided the kitchen from the living room.

Stopping in the middle of the kitchen, she let her hands relax on the wheels of the chair, grinning like a child who'd just given her teacher the slip. She'd been staying here for almost two weeks and this was the first time she'd managed to get up before Gabe. It seemed a sort of triumph. Of course, he'd worked until after midnight the night before, so she'd had a definite edge.

But she'd learned to enjoy what few successes she could. God knows, there hadn't been many of them lately. She rubbed absently at the aching muscles in her arms, her eyes on her unresponsive legs.

Two weeks out of the hospital, and all she had to show for it was a growing set of muscles in her arms. As she'd told Diane, she was going to have an upper torso like Arnold Swarzennegger and a lower body like PeeWee Herman in a few more weeks.

Diane had laughed, but was quick to say that in a few more weeks, she'd no doubt be walking again. Charity had smiled and let her sister think the words were reassuring. The truth was, it was getting harder and harder to believe that she was going to walk again.

"Stop it," she muttered out loud. It was thoughts like that that had kept her awake most of the night. Those same thoughts led to nothing but despair. She *had* to believe she was going to walk again. If she didn't hold on to that hope, she wasn't sure she could go on.

Drawing a deep breath, she squared her shoulders. It was going to be a wonderful day and she was going to enjoy it if it killed her. Her determination made Charity smile. That was a great attitude: have fun or die.

Still smiling, she wheeled her chair over to the counter. Coffee would help her mood. Nothing like a little caffeine to get the blood moving. Too little sleep, too much worrying, she scolded herself as she put the filter in place and scooped coffee into it.

A few minutes later the heady scent of brewing coffee filled the kitchen, lightening her mood. Life couldn't be a total loss as long as she could make a decent cup of coffee. Of course, she could only manage that much because Gabe had rearranged his kitchen to make things more accessible to her.

But that was dwelling on the negative, she reminded herself briskly. And she had to try and remember the positive. Like how kind Gabe had been. And how lucky she was to have a friend like him. Because he'd definitely become a friend these past weeks, and she believed that he felt the same way about her.

Charity poured herself a cup of rich, dark coffee, cradling it between her palms for a moment, as if the warmth of the cup could chase away the inner chill that never seemed far away these days.

Sipping the coffee, she suddenly thought that the perfect accompaniment to an early-morning cup of coffee would be a muffin, fresh and warm from the oven. A quick search of the cupboards told her that muffins were not among the things that Gabe stocked, not even a box of muffin mix. But he did have all the ingredients to make them from scratch.

Charity hesitated. One thing she'd learned was that the average kitchen was not set up for someone trapped in a wheelchair. The counters were too high, the majority of cupboards were out of reach. Other than making herself a sandwich or heating a can of soup, she hadn't tried to do any cooking.

Gabe had been cooking dinner. Or Diane brought something with her that could be reheated. Once Jay had ordered a pizza and joined them for dinner. Diane had stayed that night, and she and Jay had taken verbal shots at each other all night.

Maybe she should just forget about muffins, Charity thought uneasily. Or she could view it as a challenge, her more adventuresome side suggested. A chance to prove that she wasn't completely helpless. Think how nice it would be to present Gabe with homemade muffins fresh from the oven.

He'd done so much for her. She knew that he felt as if there was nothing he could do for her that would make up for the fact that it was his bullet that had injured her. But she didn't feel that way, and it would be a pleasant change to be on the giving side. Muffins could hardly compare to his opening his home to a virtual stranger, but it was the best she could offer at the moment.

She found a recipe in the one cookbook Gabe owned and began to methodically gather ingredients. A bowl, measuring spoons wedged in the back of a drawer, baking powder, sugar, eggs and milk—all were neatly lined up on the counter. The only thing she was missing was the flour.

She reached up to catch the bottom of an upper cabinet door with her fingertips, tugging it open.

There was the flour, sitting smugly on the bottom shelf, just a few inches back from the edge. Charity stretched her arm up, but she could just brush the side of the canister.

She scowled up at the cabinet. She had everything she needed to make muffins but the flour, and she wasn't about to be stymied now. She'd started this to prove that she wasn't totally helpless. She couldn't give up at the first obstacle.

She set the brake on the wheelchair so it couldn't slide out from under her. Bracing her left arm on the counter, she levered her body up, stretching her right arm toward the elusive flour. Her left arm trembled under her weight, but she was determined not to give up.

Her fingers closed around the canister, and she grinned, but it was to be a fleeting triumph. Just as she tugged the canister off the shelf, her left arm caved in under the strain. Startled, she cried out as her arm collapsed, depositing her roughly back into the chair.

She lost her grip on the metal canister, which fell to the counter, somehow losing its lid in the process, bouncing off the carton of eggs and then tumbling against the milk carton. Charity made a futile grab for the canister as it rolled off the counter and onto the floor, spreading a dusty white cloud behind it.

For an instant all she could do was stare at the disaster. There was flour everywhere. All over the counters, all over the floor, all over her. She didn't doubt that the eggs were all broken and there was a pool of milk spreading across the counter in a slow white tide.

"What happened?" Gabe, no doubt alerted by the crashing of the canister, skidded into the kitchen doorway, clad in a pair of briefs and carrying a .38.

A quick glance was enough to show him that Charity was not in danger, and he slid the gun back into its holster.

"Are you okay?" He set the holster down out of reach of the flour that was still drifting through the air and moved toward her. "Charity?"

She said nothing. She couldn't have gotten words out past the choking knot in her throat. It was a simple little task. She hadn't been trying to run a marathon or lift a Volkswagon. She'd just wanted to prove that she wasn't completely helpless.

"Charity? Are you okay?" He'd stopped next to the wheelchair, his bare feet leaving footprints on the flour-dusted floor. She saw his hand come out, and she jerked back as if his touch would burn.

"Don't touch me!" she snapped.

She tried to move the chair back, wanting only to put distance between herself and Gabe's kindness. But the brake was still on and her quick twist of the wheels did nothing but sting her palms. It was the final straw. Not only had she proven—to herself and the entire world—that she was too helpless even to feed herself, but now she couldn't even run her damned wheelchair.

"No, I am not okay," she said tightly. Her hands were clenched into fists in her lap. "I can't walk. I'm paralyzed and I'll probably always be paralyzed."

"Don't say that!"

"Why not?" she cried, her eyes filling with hot tears. "It's the truth! Everyone keeps telling me to have patience, that the feeling will come back in my legs. Well, it hasn't come back. It's never coming back. I'm going to be stuck in this damned chair for the rest of my life."

Tears blurring her vision, she pounded her fists against her thighs, feeling the impact only in her hands. "I hate my legs! I hate them. I hate them." Her voice cracked on a sob.

"Stop it!" Gabe crouched down beside the chair, catching her hands in his. "Stop talking like that."

"Why? It's the truth. I'm never going to walk again. I know it."

"You don't know anything of the kind," he barked, his fingers tightening over hers. "You're scared and you're frustrated but you're going to get past this and you're going to keep on fighting."

"No, I'm not. I'm tired of fighting." It was nothing more than the truth. All the anger had gone out of her, leaving her weary and hopeless. She let her hands stay in his because it was too much of an effort to pull them away. What difference did it make whether or not he held her hands? What difference did anything make?

"I'm paralyzed and I might as well start accepting it."

Gabe dropped her hands, reaching up to catch her shoulders in his, giving her a quick shake. Charity's startled green eyes met his, almost pure gold with emotion.

"If you say that one more time, I'm going to shake you until your teeth rattle," he told her. His tone was so fierce that she believed him.

"It's true," she whispered, her eyes dropping away from his.

"No, it's not." One hand left her shoulder to cup her chin, tilting her face up until she was forced to meet his eyes. "You're going to walk again. You just have to be patient."

"I'm sick of being patient." She would have turned her head away but he refused to release her, holding her as much with the strength of his gaze as with his grip on her chin.

"You're going to walk again, Charity." He said each word slowly and distinctly, his eyes steady on hers, willing her to believe him, to believe in herself.

"You don't know that," she muttered.

"Sure I do. Have any of the doctors told you differently? Have any of them said you won't walk?"

"No."

"Then what makes you think that's the case?"

"It's been so long, Gabe. And I still can't feel anything." Despite her determination not to cry again, new tears burned her eyes.

"I know." He slid his hand to the back of her neck, drawing her forward until her forehead rested against his. The despair in her eyes, in her voice, broke his heart. He'd have traded places with her in an instant if he were given the chance.

It was like acid in his gut to see her cry and know the tears were his doing. It was his mistake that had put her in the wheelchair she hated so passionately. Part of his bullet was still lodged near her spine. And if, God forbid, she never walked again, it would be because of him.

It was hard enough to see her struggling to stay cheerful, keeping the fear at bay by pretending it didn't exist. But it was ten times worse to see her like this, so full of despair.

"I know you're going to walk again, Charity," he said huskily. "If you don't believe the doctors, believe me. You're too strong to give up."

"I don't feel strong," she said on a sigh. But that wasn't quite true. With Gabe holding her, she did feel strong.

"You can't give up. You've got too much fight for that."

"Maybe." But he'd won and they both knew it. Her momentary urge to give up the battle was gone, chased away by his determination. "I'm sorry I acted like such an idiot."

"You're entitled to act like an idiot, once in a while."

"Gee, thanks."

"You're welcome." He drew back, smiling into her eyes.

Charity returned the smile, feeling her heart beat a little faster. It didn't seem fair that he should be so attractive first thing in the morning.

"You have flour on your face," Gabe said, brushing his fingers over her cheek. She felt the light touch shiver through her.

"So do you." She drew one finger across the light dusting of powder on his cheek.

Their eyes met and suddenly neither of them was smiling. A fine tension hummed between them, an awareness that couldn't be ignored.

"You know, you have the most beautiful smile." He brushed his thumb over her mouth, stealing her breath away.

"I do?"

"I think half the reason I was buying those crystals was because it gave me an excuse to come into the store and see you smile."

"It was?" His words stole what little breath his touch had left her. "You thought about me?"

"More than I liked to admit. I could have bought those little animals somewhere else and paid less for them, you know." His thumb stroked across her lower lip and her mouth parted.

"I didn't know."

"But they just didn't look as beautiful as they did when you were holding them."

Gabe leaned forward . . . to kiss her? And did she move to meet him?

A car backfired on the street outside, the explosion of sound shattering the fine tension of the moment. Charity sat back in her chair and Gabe eased back onto his heels, his hands sliding away from her. She felt an actual pang of loss.

Gabe looked away, groping for something to break the tension that still hummed between them. For the first time he really absorbed the disaster that was the kitchen.

"What were you trying to do?"

"Make muffins?" Charity offered, her eyes following his to the flour-strewn counters and floor. Anything was safer than looking at the long body clad in nothing but a pair of plain white briefs.

"I think you're supposed to use a bowl," he suggested, his eyes settling on the counter where milk and egg had mixed with the flour.

"No. Really?" Charity widened her eyes in shock.

"Well, I'm not sure, but it seems to me that it might be a little easier." Gabe stood up and Charity jerked her eyes away from him. She wished he'd go and put a robe on. And she wished he'd stay just as he was.

She cleared her throat, banishing thoughts of cool sheets and Gabe's lean body stretched out next to her. "I guess I'll have to keep that in mind," she said, keeping her tone light.

"You look like an extra in a haunted house movie," he said, after studying her for a moment.

"Do I?" She brought her hand up to her face, drawing it away covered in flour. Her clothes were also dusted with white powder.

"You know, maybe it's a little late to mention this, but I don't think I own a muffin pan."

Charity raised her head to look at him. "You mean, even if I hadn't made this mess, there wouldn't have been anything to bake the muffins in?"

"I think I've got a loaf pan," he offered with an apologetic shrug.

"A loaf of muffins?"

"Well, a loaf is better than none," he said seriously. The tuck that appeared in his cheek matched the laughter in his eyes.

Charity returned his smile. A few minutes ago she'd felt as if she might never have anything to smile about again. But Gabe had made it impossible for her to hold on to her depression. He'd buoyed her up again, given her the determination to keep fighting.

"Thank you, Gabe."

"For what?" He'd been dusting flour from his hands, and her quiet words brought his questioning eyes to hers. "For not having a muffin pan?"

"No. For making me laugh. For giving me a place to stay. For... being there." She lifted her shoulders in a shrug. Her eyes dropped away from his, suddenly afraid that she was starting to sound maudlin.

There was a moment of silence and then Gabe reached out and stroked his fingers over her cheek. "You don't owe me any thanks, Charity. Believe me. But if you want to thank me, just don't quit fighting."

"I won't."

Charity looked up into his eyes, feeling the light touch all through her body. If he kept looking at her like that, she'd probably promise to drag herself over hot coals. Gabe drew his hand away and Charity lowered her eyes, afraid of what he might see if she continued to look at him.

It was just the circumstances, she reminded herself. She certainly wasn't doing anything stupid... like falling in love with Gabriel London.

"DON'T MISUNDERSTAND ME, I have nothing against fashion." Jay reached for a second piece of pizza.

"You just think anyone involved in it is an airhead and a parasite," Diane ground out, her eyes spitting fire.

"I didn't say that." His tone was perfectly polite but somehow managed to convey his opinion—his low opinion—quite well.

"Have another glass of wine, Diane?" That was Charity, doing her best to pour oil—or in this case, a cheap Chianti—on troubled waters.

"Thank you." Diane barely glanced at her sister as she bit into a slice of pizza with a fervor that made Charity suspect she'd rather be biting into Jay Baldwin.

Seeking help, Charity met Gabe's eyes, but he looked more wickedly amused than concerned. She had to admit that there was a certain humor in the situation. She'd never seen anyone whose mere presence could annoy her sister so.

Maybe it was the fact that Jay was so blatantly immune to Diane's beauty. Not that Diane was overly vain, but her face and body had been turning heads since puberty. Charity suspected that it piqued her a bit to find Jay so indifferent.

Whatever the reason, the two of them were like oil and water or, more accurately, like the Gingham Dog and the Calico Cat. If they were left in a room alone, Charity wouldn't have been surprised to come back and find they'd torn each other to pieces. It seemed only the presence of witnesses that kept them from each other's throats.

"Fashion is a very important part of society," Diane said to no one in particular. "You can tell a lot about someone by the way they dress."

"It seems to me to be rather shallow to judge people by the clothes on their backs," Jay said, speaking
apparently to his glass of wine.

"Well, not all of us are gifted with the ability to read
people's minds," Diane said with awful sarcasm.
"Some of us have to rely on external clues."

Jay's eyes skimmed over her emerald-green silk top
and the chunky earrings that would have looked too
heavy on anyone else but managed to look exotic and
interesting on Diane. He took note of her carefully
tousled hair and perfectly manicured nails. A quick
sweeping glance and then he returned his attention to
the half-eaten pizza.

"With some people, the external is all there is."

There was a moment of taut silence. Diane sat back
in her chair. Her mouth opened and then shut as she
sought the words to express the anger that turned her
eyes emerald green.

"Have you heard from Brian?" Charity asked,
thrusting herself verbally between the two combat-
ants.

"What do you think of the Dodgers this year?"
Gabe spoke simultaneously.

For the rest of the meal, Jay and Diane spoke to
each other only when absolutely necessary and then
with scrupulous politeness.

"I don't know what it is with those two," Charity
said as the door closed behind her sister. Jay had left
soon after the pizza was finished. He had to be at the

office early. Diane had lingered, playing a desultory game of checkers with her sister.

"Hate at first sight," Gabe suggested, coming back into the living room and sinking onto the sofa. "Instant incompatibility."

"It must be. Diane thinks Jay is an uptight prig." She set the checkers in their box, folding up the game board to go on top of them.

"Jay thinks she's a complete airhead, so I'd guess they're about even."

"It's strange. I think Jay is the first man I've ever seen who didn't fall for Diane the minute he saw her."

"She's a beautiful woman," Gabe agreed.

"Yes, she is." Charity slid the lid on the box of checkers with a snap.

Gabe picked up a magazine and opened it. Charity wheeled her chair over to a low cupboard and slid the checkers box back into place.

Of course he thought Diane was beautiful. She *was* beautiful. She clicked the cupboard door shut, resisting the urge to slam it. She was glad he liked Diane. Glad Diane liked him. Think how uncomfortable it would have been if Diane were at odds with him as she was with Jay.

And if Gabe wanted to date her sister? The thought brought a sharp stab of pain to her chest that she promptly dismissed as too much rich food. That would be just fine, too. And all she'd need was someplace to celebrate while Gabe and Diane were out together. Someplace like a haunted crypt or maybe a nice, dank root cellar.

Not that she'd be jealous or anything. After all, it would be foolish to be jealous of her sister dating her friend. And that's all Gabe was to her. Just a friend.

Now if only she could convince her heart of that.

Chapter Nine

In the week following the flour fiasco and Jay and Diane's near fistfight over the pizza, Charity approached her physical therapy sessions with new determination. It was a battle she had to win.

There was a new closeness in her relationship with Gabe. He'd seen her without the cheerful facade she kept firmly in place for the rest of the world. Charity had faced her despair and realized that admitting to fear wasn't the same as giving in to it.

The physical therapist came by three days a week, putting Charity's legs through a series of exercises designed to keep the muscles from atrophying from lack of use. Diane drove from her studio in Beverly Hills three days a week to help her sister go through a simpler series of exercises.

Charity felt guilty about taking Diane away from her work, but need outweighed guilt. With every day that passed without any movement in her legs, the knot in her stomach grew just a bit larger, a bit harder to ignore. All the reassurance in the world that her body just needed time to heal, wasn't enough to drive away the fears that sometimes kept her awake at night.

During the day she could keep her fears at bay. She tried to keep busy, doing what housework she could, reading, watching television, teaching herself to knit. She couldn't have said just what she was making, but anything that filled her time and occupied her mind was something to be treasured.

It wasn't during the day that her fears threatened to overwhelm her. It was in the hours just before dawn when she'd wake up and there was nothing there to distract her. Hovering in the darkness between night and day, her fears had full rein.

Staring at a darkened ceiling, she tried to imagine spending the rest of her life in a wheelchair. She told herself briskly that many people managed to live happy, fulfilled lives with handicaps much greater than a simple loss of mobility.

She'd read articles about people who refused to let a handicap destroy their lives. It was so much a matter of attitude. You had to make up your mind that life was to be lived, no matter what.

But all the pep talks in the world couldn't drive away the fear that gnawed at her. She clung to her doctor's assurances that there was no reason she wouldn't walk again, but even those began to sound hollow at four o'clock in the morning.

More than once she reached for the little brass bell Gabe had placed by her bed. If she rang it, he'd come in and chase the fears away. Just having him near would force them into perspective. But she never picked up the bell.

Her emotions were already too wrapped up in Gabriel London. A few weeks ago he'd been nothing more than an attractive man who occasionally shopped in the jewelry store where she worked. In a short space of time, he'd rescued her from gunmen, brightened her otherwise tedious stay in the hospital and become her roommate and her friend. Now she was very much afraid that he might become something more.

She already depended on him too much—for companionship and support. She couldn't ask him to chase away her night fears, though she didn't doubt that he'd do it without complaint.

So she lay awake, battling the doubts and fears alone, determined that they wouldn't beat her. So far she was winning the fight.

CHARITY LOOKED UP as a shadow blocked the sun. She'd been sitting by the pool, staring at the cool blue water. Diane had called to say that her car was giving her problems and she didn't dare make the trip from Beverly Hills to Pasadena.

Charity had assured her that she could skip their session for today. The therapist would be by tomorrow. A small voice suggested that the exercise sessions didn't seem to be doing any good, anyway—what difference did it make if she skipped one? But she suppressed the negative thought.

At least the therapy sessions made her feel as if she was doing something. They gave her something concrete to do toward her recovery. And she was determined to make a recovery.

"Ready for a swim?"

Gabe moved so that he was standing in front of her. Before, he'd been nothing more than a silhouette against the sun. Without the sun in her eyes, Charity had a full view of him.

He was wearing nothing but a pair of black swim trunks—nothing exotic—just perfectly ordinary swim trunks. She swallowed hard. It wasn't as if she hadn't seen him without a shirt before. Or for that matter, without his pants. The morning she'd coated the kitchen with flour, he'd been wearing only briefs, which certainly hadn't concealed any more than the trunks did.

But that morning she'd been more than a little distraught, and though she'd noticed his lack of clothing, it hadn't had the impact it was having now.

She swallowed again, her eyes traveling over muscled shoulders and chest, following the dusting of curling hair that arrowed across his stomach to disappear into the top of his trunks. Her eyes skittered over that all-too-tantalizing garment to trail down a pair of long, muscled legs, ending at bare feet planted solidly on the concrete that surrounded the pool.

She kept her eyes on those feet. It was safer than looking anywhere else.

"Charity? Did you fall asleep on me?"

Asleep? Not likely. Not with her pulse doing double-time. She blinked and slowly raised her eyes to his face. He was giving her a quizzical look, his brows raised in question.

"I'm not asleep." She cleared her throat, trying to look as if she weren't wondering what it would feel like to run her fingers through the hair on his chest.

"Good. I thought I'd lost you for a minute there."

"Sorry, I guess my mind wandered off. What did you say?"

"I asked if you were ready for a swim."

"A swim?" She looked from him to the pool and then back at him. "You mean, you and me? In the pool?"

"That's where people generally swim. I know Diane can't make it today, and I don't have anything else to do this afternoon."

Charity was already shaking her head. "I don't think so." It was one thing to let the therapist or Diane help her. It was something else altogether to think of getting into the water with Gabe.

"Come on. I'm a good swimmer." He crouched down in front of her, his smile coaxing. "You can trust me."

"I do trust you."

"Then what's the problem?"

"You must have something you'd rather do. You don't want to waste your time watching me flounder around."

"I told you, I don't have anything else to do. Come on, you don't want to miss a session, do you? The weather is perfect for swimming. It's over ninety. Think how good the water would feel."

Charity hesitated, looking from his coaxing smile to the water lapping quietly in the pool. It was true, the water would feel wonderful. And the pool was the only place where she felt almost normal. The buoyancy of the water helped to compensate for her useless legs, giving her a temporary illusion of normalcy.

"You don't know any of the exercises," she said.

"You can show me what to do."

She hesitated. It was true that the thought of getting into the cool water was tempting. But she wasn't at all sure she was prepared to have Gabe's hands on her. She never gave a thought to the fact that Diane or the therapist was touching her, but she couldn't imagine being so indifferent to Gabe's touch.

"Come on." Gabe sat back on his heels in front of her, his smile reassuring. "I'll take good care of you. You couldn't be in safer hands."

"Really?" She felt herself weakening under the combined temptation of the pool and his eyes.

"Sure. I was a lifeguard one summer in Santa Monica."

"Did you ever get in the water, or did you just sit up there in your little tower ogling all the girls in their bikinis?"

"I was devoted to my job," he said self-righteously. "The bikinis were merely a side benefit."

"Right." Charity's expression conveyed her doubts about this noble claim.

"Are you going to get in the pool or just sit there casting aspersions on my character?"

Charity hesitated, but she knew what the end result was going to be. She was acting like an idiot. Gabe was nothing but a friend. It made no difference whether it was him helping her with her exercises or Diane. Okay, so Diane didn't have all those sexy muscles and Diane didn't put butterflies in her stomach. But those were minor details.

So Gabe was an attractive man. That didn't mean anything.

Nothing except that he made her heart beat too fast and her palms feel damp.

"Is it that hard to make a decision?" he asked, sounding vaguely hurt.

"No. No, of course not. I really appreciate the offer. If you're sure you don't mind."

"I don't mind."

A few minutes later Charity was chest-deep in the pool. Water wings helped keep her afloat. The first time she'd gotten in the pool, she'd been terrified. She'd felt completely helpless outside the hated security of the wheelchair.

It hadn't taken long for her to come to appreciate the benefits of working in the pool. With the water supporting her, it was almost possible to forget that her legs didn't work.

For all that he'd used humor to coax her into the pool, Gabe was completely serious when it came to the simple exercises she usually did in the water.

Charity had been nervous about having him touch her, but it wasn't long before she genuinely forgot whose hands were guiding and supporting her. There was nothing personal or sexual in his touch, nothing to hint that he even saw her as female.

In fact his attitude was so impersonal Charity wondered if she should be insulted.

But once the official reason for spending a hot afternoon in the water had been satisfied, Gabe's serious demeanor vanished.

"You know, if I'd known you guys were having this much fun out here, I'd have made it a point to get more afternoons off."

He let Charity float free, the water wings supporting her weight. He stretched out on his back, closing his eyes against the sun that poured down out of a cloudless sky.

"You're lucky to have a pool like this," Charity said, tilting her face to the sun. "There's a pool at my apartment building but it's small. When the weather is like this, everyone crowds into it.''

"My grandparents put this pool in because they wanted my mother to be an Olympic swimmer.''

"And was she?'' Charity was suddenly aware of how little she knew about him.

"No. She never made it that far.''

"Were her parents disappointed?''

"Not to the point of disowning her. After I was born, they had hopes for me.''

"Did you compete?''

"In school. But I never had the kind of drive it takes to go for the Olympics. You've got to want it more than anything else.''

"And you wanted to be a police officer.''

"Well, first I wanted to be a fireman. That was when I was five. Then I was going to be a cowboy. When I was about twelve, I was going to be the next Hank Aaron.''

"So when did you decide to be a cop?''

"About the time I got out of college and realized that there were limited choices for someone with a degree in history.''

"You could have gone into teaching.''

"I thought about it but I never saw myself standing in a classroom, trying to drum history into a bunch of kids who'd rather be anywhere else.''

"So what made you decide to be a cop?'' Charity persisted.

"Would you believe an ad on television? I was trying to figure out what the hell to do with a history degree and the rest of my life, and I saw this ad about the joys of being a security guard. But I decided to go them one better and entered the academy."

"You must like it, to have stayed with it for twelve years."

"It has its moments," he said slowly.

"You sound doubtful." Charity shot him a quick look.

"I don't think *like* is exactly the word I'd use," he said. "It can be incredibly fulfilling and incredibly frustrating, all at the same time. It's great when you help someone or arrest someone who's hurt other people. But often as not, they're back on the street in a matter of weeks, sometimes in a matter of hours. It tends to shake your faith in the system."

"You sound a little burned out."

"Sometimes," he admitted, hearing the weariness in his voice.

"What about your parents? Where are they?" Seeing Gabe's eyes were closed, Charity let her eyes linger on him, enjoying the sight of his relaxed body. He might have been asleep but for the occasional movement of his hands through the water, keeping him afloat.

"Mom died eight years ago and Dad moved to Wyoming. He's raising horses."

"Sounds nice."

"He's been after me to join him."

"Are you going to?"

"I don't know." Gabe was surprised to hear his own words. He'd convinced himself that the idea of moving to Wyoming to join his dad was nothing more than a premature mid-life crisis. Shaking his head, he changed the subject.

"What about you? What do you plan to do when you grow up?" He shot her a quick grin.

"I don't know. I guess I'm not all that ambitious. I liked working at the jewelry store. Mr. Hoffman visited me in the hospital and told me I can come back whenever I want."

"Will you?"

"I don't know." She sighed. "I just never had a driving ambition to be anything in particular. Diane always knew she wanted to design clothes. Becoming a model was just a way to earn money and get the connections she needed. And Brian is such a brain that he's managed to work in two or three life goals already. Sometimes it makes me tired just to think about it."

"And what do you want?"

"Besides being able to walk again?" She lifted her shoulders. "Not much. A home. Someone special in my life. Maybe a child." She shrugged again, her smile self-deprecating. "Nothing all that exciting, I'm afraid."

"Excitement isn't all it's cracked up to be. I think what you want is pretty much what everyone wants. It's just that these days we all make it so much more complicated than it has to be."

Conversation slowed after that. With the hot sun beating down and the gentle motion of the water lulling them, talk seemed too much of an effort. A jet flew over, so high it was little more than a shadow against the bright blue of the sky.

Charity watched it, wondering where it was headed. Wouldn't it be wonderful to be on that plane, going somewhere far away, leaving all her troubles behind. Her mouth twisted. That was funny—trying to run away from paralysis.

But she didn't feel particularly amused. She felt her relaxed mood draining away, threatening to turn into depression. But not today. Not right now. She wasn't going to think about her unresponsive legs or the possibility that she might not walk again.

Gabe gave a startled gasp as a miniature tidal wave of cold water splashed onto his sun-warmed stomach. Folding up like a pocket knife, he went under but only for a second.

He surfaced instantly, tossing his hair back from his face, his eyes seeking the source of the pool's sudden turbulence. Charity looked back at him, her green eyes wide and innocent, but he wasn't fooled.

"You tried to drown me."

"*Moi?* I wouldn't do anything like that."

"Then where did that wave come from?"

"Perhaps an asteroid fell in the pool?" Charity suggested.

"Doesn't seem likely." He paddled forward until he could stand on the bottom. Charity used her arms to ease herself backward in the water.

"How about an earthquake? They can slosh the water right out of a pool."

"Odd that the water only seemed to slosh over me." He advanced and she retreated.

"Maybe it was a very small earthquake. Localized." She bit her lip to hold back a smile.

"With an epicenter right under my pool?" Gabe thought he'd never seen her look more beautiful than she did right now, her eyes sparkling with mischief, her face lightly flushed with sun.

"Maybe you have a fault line under your pool," she offered. "Southern California is riddled with them. Maybe there's a branch of the San Andreas fault right under us now."

"Maybe. Or maybe it wasn't an earthquake at all." He stopped in front of her, scowling fiercely. But his eyes were laughing, and the tuck in one cheek told her he was trying not to smile.

"Well, if it wasn't an earthquake and it wasn't an asteroid, what do you think it might have been?"

"I have my theories," he said darkly. He drew back his hand and Charity had only a moment to draw in a quick breath before he skimmed it across the surface, sending a sheet of water ahead of it. Her eyes squeezed shut as the water cascaded over her face.

"That was totally uncalled for," she protested, wiping the water out of her eyes.

"I'm sorry." His grin made the apology seem less than sincere. "I have this terrible twitch in my arm sometimes. Did I splash you?"

"Not at all." She brought both hands together in front of her, pushing them forward in a movement that simultaneously sent a wave of water toward Gabe's smiling face and pushed her back out of reach.

It was not, perhaps, the most vigorous game of water warfare she'd ever played, limited as her movements were. The game consisted in large part of her trying to splash Gabe before he could duck. The fact that he could have easily swum out of reach seemed irrelevant.

For the first time since the shooting, Charity completely forgot about her injury. Buoyed by the water, bathed in the warmth of Gabe's laughter, she felt young, happy and, most of all, normal. This was one place where it didn't matter whether or not her legs worked. Or so she almost managed to convince herself.

Gabe had ducked underwater, and she turned to look for him. But she hadn't realized how close to the edge she was. The side of the pool loomed inches away, startling her into flailing backward, off balance, her movements clumsy.

For an instant she sank under the surface of the pool. The water closed over her head, and for one horrible moment she felt totally helpless. She'd been swimming since she was a child, and she couldn't possibly have counted the number of times Diane or Brian had dunked her or she'd gone underwater on her own.

But this time was different. This time there'd be no pushing up off the bottom, no quick kick to send her upward into the air, as there would have been if she'd had the use of her legs.

The water wings were forgotten. The fact that Gabe would hardly stand by and let her drown was forgotten. For that one horrible moment she was completely alone and completely helpless.

The water wings brought her to surface almost instantly and she drew in a gasping breath. But it wasn't enough to be back on the surface. She wanted out of the deceptively inviting water. She wanted the safety of her wheelchair, no matter how hateful it was.

Gabe was standing less than two feet away, the water lapping just short of his collarbone. He must have seen the panic on her face because his smile disappeared and he reached out to catch her arms.

"What's wrong? Are you in pain?"

Charity wrapped her fingers around his forearms, clinging to the sturdy support. The five feet of water beneath her suddenly felt endless.

"I want to get out," she said breathlessly.

"What happened?" Unconsciously Gabe drew her closer, his hands sliding up to her shoulders.

"I want out," she repeated. Near hysteria tightened her voice. "Now."

"Okay. It's all right." Gabe's voice dropped to a soothing murmur. His hands shifted and Charity clutched at him, her nails digging into his arms.

"Don't let go of me!"

Immediately he had her wrapped against him, his arms strong and hard against her back. "I won't let go. What happened?"

"I went under." She pressed her forehead to his shoulder, struggling to tamp down the panic that threatened to choke her.

"I was right here," he reminded her, one hand moving soothingly up and down her spine.

"I couldn't breathe and I couldn't swim." Tears burned at the back of her eyes.

"I wouldn't let anything happen to you."

"I know." With his arms holding her close, Charity felt the panic receding. Of course he wouldn't have let her drown.

"I just felt so helpless," she whispered.

Gabe's arms tightened around her for a moment, and then he eased her back far enough to cup one hand under her chin, tilting her face up to his.

"I'm never going to let anything happen to you, Charity."

She closed her eyes as his thumb brushed across her cheek. His mouth followed the same path, soft kisses drying the tears from her skin. Charity shivered.

Any remaining wisps of fear were rapidly edged out by the warmth of his kisses. His mouth touched the corner of hers and she forgot how to breathe. For the space of several heartbeats neither of them moved.

Charity's hands shifted restlessly on his shoulders. As if it was the signal he'd been waiting for, Gabe's mouth settled over hers.

What had begun as gentle comfort turned to white heat in the space of a breath. His lips were cool and damp, but there was nothing cool about the feelings they stirred.

Charity's hands slid upward, her fingers disappearing into his thick wet hair. Gabe's hand tightened in her hair, tilting her head to deepen the kiss. When he drew back, Charity could feel his heart pounding against her breast. No doubt he could feel her heartbeat, the rhythm quick and hard.

She dragged her eyes open to stare up at him. His face was so close she could see the tiny gold lines that radiated out through the green of his eyes. Those eyes were searching her face, looking for something. She didn't need a mirror to know what he saw. Her eyes must be as dazed as she felt, her cheeks flushed, her mouth half-parted as if in invitation.

It was an invitation he didn't hesitate to accept, and Charity let out a soft sigh of pleasure as his mouth closed over hers again. His tongue dragged along her lower lip. With a delicious shudder she opened her mouth to him, her tongue coming up to twine with his.

The sun beat down on them, but its heat paled before the sudden fire burning between them. It was as if all the tensions of the past weeks had suddenly found release.

One of Gabe's hands stroked up and down her spine, leaving hot trails of awareness everywhere he touched. Charity drew closer, pressing herself against him as if he could somehow absorb her into himself.

Never in her life had she experienced a hunger like the one suddenly burning in the pit of her stomach. She couldn't get enough of him—his touch, his taste, the feel of his mouth, the silkiness of his hair beneath her fingers. And Gabe seemed to feel a similar hunger.

Afterward she wondered what would have happened if a shriek of laughter hadn't suddenly sliced through the still afternoon. The laughter was followed by a loud splash from next door. Obviously the neighbors were taking advantage of their pool.

The sound cut between them like a hot knife through butter. Gabe jerked back, his eyes locked in hers, his chest expanding as he drew a deep breath. Charity stared at him for a moment and then looked away, afraid of what he might see in her eyes; afraid of what she might see if she looked in her heart.

A light breeze skimmed across the water, and she shivered as it touched her wet shoulders.

"I...I think I'd like to get out now," she murmured without looking at him.

His hands were on her upper arms, and she felt his fingers tighten for a moment as if he might have protested. But if the thought occurred to him, he changed his mind. Without a word he guided her to the edge of the pool.

Charity gasped, her fingers clutching his shoulders for balance as he put his hands to her waist and lifted her to sit on the warm concrete.

She tried not to notice the way the water cascaded off his back and shoulders as he heaved himself out of the pool next to her. She tried not to notice how easily he lifted her, easing her down in the wheelchair. Most of all she tried not to notice how badly she wanted to run her fingers over the broad muscles of his chest.

Seated once again in the wheelchair, she felt the loss of that momentary illusion of normalcy the pool had given her. Staring down at her legs, she reminded herself that Gabe wouldn't have looked at her twice if it hadn't been for the shooting. And he wouldn't have kissed her if she hadn't been wrapped around him like a wet dishrag.

But the reasons for the kiss weren't as important as making sure that he knew she wasn't expecting anything to change because of it. She reached up to take the towel Gabe was handing her, forcing a wide smile.

"Well, that was certainly a surprise." Yes, that was just the right note of cheerful unconcern, she thought.

"I suppose you could call it that," he said slowly, picking up a second towel and rubbing it slowly over his chest. Charity dragged her eyes away from the motion, scrubbing her own towel over her arms.

"And you don't have to worry about me thinking this changes anything," she continued.

"I don't?"

"Of course not. It's my legs that don't work, not my brain, Gabe." She shot him a quick, smiling glance, her eyes darting away almost before they reached his face.

"I never thought there was anything wrong with your brain."

"Good. Because there isn't. I know what just happened."

Gabe finished drying his torso and then draped the towel around his neck, holding one end in each hand, his gaze questioning as he looked down at her.

"You want to explain it to me?"

"Proximity." She threw him another of those quick, meaningless smiles.

"Proximity." He repeated evenly.

"That's right. I *was* practically plastered to you," she said, as if he might have forgotten just how close they'd been.

Not bloody likely, Gabe thought. Not when he could still feel the imprint of her slim body against his chest. Not when his hands could still feel her damp skin sliding under them. No, he didn't need to be reminded of how close they'd been.

"Proximity," he said again, his voice expressionless.

"That's right." Charity watched uneasily as he sat down on the end of a redwood chaise lounge.

"So you figure that I'd have kissed any woman I happened to find plastered to my chest?"

Put that way it didn't sound terribly flattering to either of them. Charity flushed and shifted uneasily in the chair.

"That's not what I meant."

"Then what did you mean?"

"It's just that we've been spending a lot of time together these past couple of weeks, what with me living in your house and all. And I know you worry about me, about my walking again, I mean."

"What does that have to do with us kissing just now?"

"Well, you haven't gone out at all. Dated, I mean." She let her voice trail off, staring miserably at the cement decking.

Gabe's brows rose. "So I kissed you because I haven't been going out with other women? That's not very flattering, Charity. It makes me sound like an oversexed moron."

"That's not what I meant." Her head jerked up, her expression worried until she caught the humor in his eyes. Her mouth curved in a rueful smile. "I didn't mean to put it quite that way."

"So you *do* think I'm an oversexed moron but you didn't want to actually say that," Gabe asked helpfully.

"Well, not the oversexed part at least."

"Gee, thanks."

"I just worry that you're putting your life on hold for me," she said on a more serious note. "You don't have to sit around with me every night. I mean, if you want to go out with...with someone, you should go."

"Maybe I like sitting around with you," he suggested. The look Charity threw him told him she certainly wasn't going to believe that, even for a moment. Gabe didn't pursue the issue.

"I just don't want you to feel like you have to hover over me. I'm doing just fine. I'm going to get my legs back," she said. The very force of her words exposed her doubts. Realizing that, she shrugged, her mouth twisting in a half smile. "And if I don't...well, at least I'll be able to park in handicapped spots without getting a ticket."

Gabe sensed she was retreating as fast as she could from the intimacy of their kiss. The unexpected surge of passion had surprised her as much as it had him. But where he had been exhilarated by the discovery, she seemed to be frightened.

Proximity. Like hell that's all it was. Proximity might have started the kiss. But it didn't explain how right she'd felt in his arms. Nor did it explain the urge he had to kiss her right now.

But this wasn't the time. He could see that quite clearly. He wouldn't force the issue. But one of these days he was going to have to show Ms. Charity Williams that proximity alone wasn't enough to spark a fire like the one that had flared between them.

Chapter Ten

"Now, you're sure you'll be okay on your own?" Gabe gave her a concerned look.

"I'll be fine," Charity assured him. "It isn't like I haven't been alone here before."

"But not at night."

"I don't think night or day makes much difference."

He shrugged into a soft corduroy jacket, still frowning. "You're sure you don't need anything before I go?"

"Nothing. Diane brought me some old Cary Grant movies. I'm going to pop some popcorn in the microwave and watch movies all evening."

"Jay is just next door if you need anything," he reminded her, as if she might forget where Jay lived.

"I know." Charity gave him what she hoped was a confident smile.

Gabe picked up his car keys but hesitated. "I won't be late."

"Stay out as late as you want," she told him.

He hovered in the doorway. "You're sure there's nothing I can get you before I leave?"

"Nothing!" she said, laughing. "Go before I call the police and have you thrown out."

"Well, if you're sure..." She picked up a pillow and held it up threateningly. "Okay, okay. I'm going. Don't forget that Jay is—"

"I know. I know. He's next door. Now get out of here."

Her exasperated smile faded as the door closed behind him. Lowering the pillow, she cradled it against her chest, listening to the sound of his car as it pulled out of the drive. The sound faded down the street and she was alone.

Not that she hadn't been alone before. As she'd pointed out to him, she'd spent a good part of most days alone. But she felt more alone now than she had since leaving the hospital. Gabe hadn't just gone out. He'd gone out on a date.

You're the one who urged him to go.

But she hadn't really expected him to take her up on it.

You told him not to let your presence interfere with his life.

But that didn't mean he had to run out and get a date two days later.

What do you care? It's not as if you're in love with him.

Of course not. She just worried about the kind of woman he might be going out with. She didn't have to be in love with Gabe to know that he was a very special man. He deserved a very special woman. What if this woman didn't appreciate how kind he was, how sensitive?

"He's only going out on a date with her," she muttered aloud. "Not marrying her."

She tossed the pillow back onto the sofa and, putting a hand on one wheel, turned the chair toward the kitchen. She wasn't going to spend the entire evening wondering about Gabe—what he was doing, who he was with. Especially not who he was with.

She was going to do exactly what she'd told Gabe she was going to do. She was going to eat too much popcorn, watch too many movies, and then she was going to go to bed and sleep soundly. She certainly wasn't going to do anything foolish, like wait up for Gabe.

THE HANDS of the small alarm clock stood straight up. Midnight. Charity rolled her head away, telling herself to go to sleep. She'd been in bed for over an hour, most of that time spent staring at the ceiling. Every time a car drove by, she tensed, waiting to see if it would pull into the drive.

It wasn't that she was waiting up for him, she told herself. It was just that she was concerned. What if he'd had an accident? Or a flat tire? Or run out of gas on the freeway?

Or decided to spend the night at his date's apartment?

She squeezed her eyes shut as if she could close out the image of Gabe holding another woman in his arms; Gabe kissing her; Gabe in bed with her.

It was none of her business. She didn't care if he was sleeping with this woman, whoever she was. Probably a bosomy brunette with big brown eyes like a cow.

Her eyes opened again to stare at the same patch of ceiling. She'd developed an intimate acquaintance with the ceiling over her bed these past few weeks. It wasn't as if, when she couldn't sleep, it was a simple thing to just get up and wander out to the kitchen.

That was another reason sleep was proving so elusive tonight. Earlier in the afternoon she'd thought she felt something in her legs. A tingling . . . faint, hardly noticeable, the sensation gone almost before she realized it was there.

She hadn't mentioned it to Gabe or to Diane when she'd come by with the tapes. She didn't want to get their hopes up. She was glad now that she hadn't said anything, because there hadn't been any repetition of the feeling, if indeed, there'd *been* any feeling.

Despite her determination not to make too much of what could be nothing, Charity couldn't help but hope. It was the first time since the shooting that she'd sensed any sign of progress.

The sound of the front door opening startled her out of her thoughts. She raised herself up on her elbows, staring at the bedroom door, listening as Gabe walked across the living room and into the hallway that led to the bedrooms.

He had to walk past her room to get to his own. Charity felt her pulse speed as she listened to his quiet footsteps. He stopped outside her door and her heart skipped a beat. She stared at the door, hardly breathing, waiting. She couldn't have said what she was waiting for.

He stood there for the space of several seconds, and Charity felt the tension in every fiber of her body. What would she say if he came in? What would he say?

When he moved on, she fell back against her pillows, drawing a deep breath. His bedroom door closed with a barely audible click, and the last of the tension drained from her.

Fool. What did you think he was going to do? Come in and declare his undying love? After he just spent the evening with a dark-eyed beauty who could walk?

The tears she refused to shed burned at the back of her eyes. It was a good thing she wasn't falling in love with Gabe.

"So, HOW WAS your date?" That was good. Just the right tone of polite interest.

"It wasn't exactly a date," Gabe said, sitting down at the table, coffee cup in hand. "Beth is the sister of one of the officers I went through the academy with. She needed an escort to a business thing."

Not a date. Charity sternly squashed the little bubble of pleasure the words gave her. It didn't matter to her one way or another if it had been a date. She wouldn't let it matter.

"I've been thinking." She stirred her spoon absently in her cereal.

"A dangerous occupation at this hour of the morning." Gabe glanced at the clock, calculating how much time he had left before he had to leave for work.

"Maybe I should find somewhere else to live."

It took a moment for her words to sink in, but when they did, his eyes jerked to her. She continued to stare at her cereal.

"Why?"

"Well, it's not really fair to you, having me dumped on you like this. I mean, when I moved in, I thought I'd be walking again in a few days."

"Let me worry about what's fair to me. And you *are* going to walk again."

"I know," she said without much conviction. "And I can't let you worry about what's fair because you probably wouldn't admit it if I was cramping your style."

"Cramping my style?" He raised his brows at the phrase. "What style are we talking about? I never knew I had a style and now it's suddenly in danger of being cramped.''

Charity gave a perfunctory smile but she returned doggedly to the subject. She'd spent a lot of hours thinking this out and she was determined to have her say.

"Well, like last night, for example."

"For an example of what?" Gabe thrust his fingers through his hair.

"If I hadn't been here, you might have brought Beth back with you."

"Not unless I wanted her brother to tear my head off. Joe is six foot four and *very* protective."

"Well, if it hadn't been Beth, you might have brought her back here," Charity pursued stubbornly.

"I'd have felt like a total fool taking someone else to Beth's party."

"I'm serious, Gabe."

"I can see that. What I don't see is what you're serious about."

"What if you wanted to bring a woman back here?"

"I don't."

"But what if you did?"

"Charity, would you stop worrying about my love life?" He left his seat and went over to where she was sitting. Turning the wheelchair away from the table, he sat back on his heels in front of her, putting himself at her eye level.

"Contrary to the popular image of swinging bachelors, I do not sleep with every woman I meet. Beth is a friend, nothing more. If I'd never met you, I still wouldn't have brought her back here. Does that satisfy you?"

"What if she wasn't just a friend?" Charity ran her thumb along the arm of the chair, keeping her eyes on the movement, rather than meeting his eyes.

"Charity, I have no desire to make love to another woman. At the moment the only woman I want is busy trying to throw me out of her life."

Charity's startled eyes swept to his, reading in their depths exasperation, amusement and...desire? She looked away.

"You don't have to be kind to me, Gabe."

"Kind?"

"Pretending you...want me," she said, getting the words out with difficulty.

"Why do you assume I'm pretending?"

"I know you feel bad about me being...like this." She gestured to her legs.

"I feel guilty as hell," he said bluntly. "But that doesn't mean I don't find you attractive."

She slanted him a quick look, an equal mix of vulnerability and doubt in her eyes.

"Charity, you're a beautiful, sexy woman. Why is it so hard to believe I'm attracted to you?"

Color flooded her face at his compliment but she was already shaking her head. "I'm not beautiful.

And I'm certainly not sexy. Especially not stuck in this thing. You're just trying to be kind.''

"Once and for all, I'm not being kind.'' Annoyance colored his voice. "*I* think you're beautiful and *I* find you very sexy.'' His hand curved around the back of her neck. Charity's startled eyes met his as he drew her forward.

"I guess maybe actions will speak louder than words,'' he murmured an instant before his mouth closed over hers.

The impact was the same as when he kissed her in the pool. She'd nearly managed to convince herself that she'd imagined the feelings that had flared up between them then. But it wasn't imagination that put hunger in Gabe's mouth.

Her hands came up to clutch at his shoulders—for balance, she told herself. Her mouth opened under the hungry demand of his, her fingers sliding upward to bury themselves in the softness of his hair.

When he broke the kiss a moment later, they were both out of breath. It was all Charity could do to keep from whimpering a protest. Her fingers left his hair reluctantly, dropping to rest on his shoulders.

Gabe drew back just until his eyes met hers. "Did that feel like I was just being kind?''

Dazed, she blinked at him as she struggled to sort out her thoughts. There hadn't been anything particularly kind about his kiss. Hunger, demand, maybe a touch of good old-fashioned lust but not kindness. She stared into his green-gold eyes. She wanted to believe that he could desire her, wanted it so much it made her wary.

"I—"

But whatever she'd been going to say was destined to remain unheard. The sharp ring of the doorbell cut through the tense moment. Charity jerked her hands from Gabe's shoulders as if she'd just been caught in some sin. Gabe ignored the bell a moment longer, his eyes holding hers.

"You think about it," he told her.

She swallowed hard and nodded. *As if she was likely to think of anything else.* The bell rang again, taking on an annoyed whine, as if transmitting the irritation of whoever was ringing it. Gabe shot her one last look before standing up.

"Who the hell could that be," he said to no one in particular, glancing at the clock. Eight o'clock on a weekday morning was hardly a prime visiting hour.

Charity didn't know who it could be. At the moment she wasn't entirely sure she knew who *she* was, let alone who might be at the door.

She watched as Gabe strode out of the kitchen. His hair was tousled where her hands had slid through it. She curled her fingers against her palm. She felt as if she was suddenly seeing the world with new eyes.

Gabe found her desirable. What an amazing thought. She wanted to explore it more fully. Roll it over in her mind and look at the idea from different angles. But not, apparently, right now.

"Where is my sister?" The angry question cut across her tangled thoughts. Brian. He'd left for Europe a couple of days before she was released from the hospital. Obviously he was back, and from the sound of his voice, not in a good mood.

She wheeled herself out of the kitchen. Gabe, Diane and Brian were just stepping from the entryway into the living room. Brian saw Charity first and crossed the room to crouch down beside her.

"Charity. How are you, honey?" In his eyes was the shock of seeing her in a wheelchair for the first time.

"I'm fine, Brian." Since he seemed reluctant to make the first move, as if afraid she might break, she looped her arms around his neck. He returned the hug with gentle ferocity and she felt tears fill her eyes. All her life Brian had been there for her.

When they were younger, he might have pulled her hair or teased her mercilessly, but he'd also been the first to defend her if some other little boy tried the same tricks. He'd visited daily while she was in the hospital. In his eyes she'd seen his frustration at not being able to make her world right.

"When did you get home?" she asked as he released her.

"Last night."

"And he was at my place bright and early this morning, demanding to see you," Diane put in acidly. Early morning was not her favorite time of day.

"Well, since no one had bothered to tell me where you were, I think my concern was not unjustified." Brian stood up and turned to glare at Diane.

"As you can see, I'm just fine." Charity spoke quickly to head off the argument she could see brewing between her siblings.

"I don't know that I see that at all."

"Well, the wheelchair is a temporary necessity," Charity said defensively, surprised by his insensitive attitude.

"I'm not talking about the wheelchair. I'm talking about your living arrangements. What are you doing here...with him?"

Charity saw Gabe's brows go up at Brian's tone but she couldn't tell whether he was annoyed or amused that Brian had managed to make him sound like Ted Bundy.

"Gabe has been very kind in letting me stay here, Brian." But he ignored her repressive tone.

"Kind!" The word exploded out of him. "Kind! Are you crazy. He's the one who shot you. You could have died."

"I didn't die, and the shooting wasn't Gabe's fault."

"Then I'd like to know whose fault it was. He's the one who pulled the trigger."

"Stop it." Charity's tone was crisp with annoyance. "It was an accident."

"Don't worry about defending me, Charity. I don't blame your brother for feeling the way he does."

"Well, that's real gracious of you," Brian said. His angry glance took any possible compliment out of the words.

"Is this a private fight, or can anyone join?" Jay stood in the doorway, his eyes questioning as he observed the tense scene.

"Who are you?" Brian demanded, ready to add him to the list of villains.

"This is Gabe's neighbor," Diane said before anyone else could answer. "I'm surprised you're not off doing good deeds somewhere," she said to Jay, her voice dripping with acid sweetness.

"I'm surprised you're out of bed this early. I'd think you'd need all the beauty sleep you can get."

Diane sucked in a quick breath, her magnificent eyes flashing in anger. Brian, dismissing Jay as unimportant to the present conflict, turned his attention to Gabe.

"I suppose you thought you could wipe the slate clean by offering my sister a place to stay. But it's not that simple. I don't know how you managed to talk her into staying with you but she's not spending another day in this house."

Gabe remained stubbornly silent. He'd slid his hands into the back pockets of his jeans and was staring at the floor, his expression impossible to see.

"Brian!" But Charity's protest was swallowed by Diane's angry voice.

"You know what I can't stand?" She glared at Jay. "I can't stand self-important prigs who think that they're more important than anyone else."

"And I suppose you think designing clothes for rich women to wear once then throw away is an important contribution to the world?" Jay shot back.

"You can't just walk away from your guilt in this," Brian said, ignoring the battle between Diane and Jay. "You're the one who pulled the trigger. You're going to have to live with that, and you can't make it all better by offering her a place to stay."

Charity lifted a hand to her head, feeling a headache starting to pound in her temples. Diane and Jay were in the midst of a full-blown argument, the subject of which she couldn't quite pin down.

They'd raised their voices, either in anger or simply to be heard over Brian's accusations. Brian had raised his voice over theirs, which brought the noise level up another notch.

Gabe offered not a word in his own defense, letting Brian's words wash over him unchallenged. His complete lack of response only fueled Brian's anger.

"You may have been able to fool my sisters into thinking you had nothing but altruistic motives, but I know better. She's moving out today. I—"

"Quiet!"

It was amazing what results could be obtained with a single word, especially when that word was shouted. All conversation came to an abrupt halt, and there was blessed silence. All eyes turned to Charity.

Diane and Brian couldn't have looked more startled if the lampshade had suddenly spoken. Jay looked surprised, though he didn't know her well enough to be as shocked as her siblings. Gabe's head jerked up, his quizzical expression quickly changing to one of amused pride.

Charity drew a deep breath, letting the quiet wash over her.

"Are you okay, Char?" That was Brian, bending over her solicitously, his expression so anxious that she promptly forgave him for trying to run her life.

"I'm fine, Brian."

"Then why did you shout?" His concern changed to puzzlement.

"It seemed like the only way to remind you all that I was still here," she said ruefully.

"What do you mean?" Diane asked, frowning. Jay slid his hands into his pockets, his expression going from puzzled to understanding.

"It's very nice to know that all of you are so concerned about me," Charity said. "I really appreciate it but I think it would be nice if someone thought to ask *me* what I wanted to do."

"Well, of course we care what you want to do," Diane said.

"Of course we do," Brian said supportively. "As soon as we get you moved out of here, we'll settle you anywhere you like."

"Maybe she doesn't want to move out," Gabe said quietly, speaking for the first time since the argument began.

"You stay out of this." Brian shot him an angry look. "If it wasn't for you, she—"

"Brian." Charity didn't shout this time but there was a steely note in her voice that made him break off instantly.

"If it wasn't for Gabe, I would be dead." She tilted her head back to fix her older brother with a stern look. "I've told him and I'll tell you. He has nothing to feel guilty about."

"You don't have to defend me," Gabe told her.

"Damn right, she doesn't." Brian caught Charity's eye and subsided.

"What *do* you want to do, Charity?" It was left to Jay to get back to the main question.

Charity threw a quick glance at Gabe before focusing her attention on the toes of her tennis shoes. She knew what she *wanted* to do. She just didn't know if it was the *smart* thing to do.

Remembering the steamy kiss she and Gabe had shared just before the doorbell rang, she wondered if the smart choice wouldn't be to let Brian move her out as quickly as possible.

But she didn't *want* to leave Gabe's house. She didn't want to leave Gabe. He'd said he found her attractive, desirable. If she left now, would she ever find out if he'd meant it?

"Charity?" Brian's prompting made her realize how long she'd been silent. The time had come to make a decision—right or wrong.

"If Gabe doesn't mind—"

"He doesn't," Gabe said, earning a fierce look from Brian.

"I'd like to stay here."

Chapter Eleven

"You know, there are moments—more than a few of them—when I have serious doubts about my suitability for this job." Gabe slammed his car door as he spoke.

Annie shut her own door with more control, sliding her partner a sympathetic glance. "You can only help people who want to be helped, Gabriel. You can't force people to do what's good for them. Nita has to make the decision to leave Lawrence herself. Then we can see about getting her some help."

"Why would she stay?" Gabe asked, his voice rough with frustration. "She's got family. They'd take her in."

"She thinks she loves him, sugar." Annie shrugged. "As long as she thinks that, she ain't goin' to leave him."

"Why would a nice kid like Nita hook up with a two-bit enforcer like Lawrence?" Gabe turned the key in the ignition, the movement so violent that Annie wouldn't have been surprised to see the key snap off.

"Maybe he seemed real romantic," she suggested as they pulled away from the curb.

Nita had probably already called her boyfriend to tell him that the cops had been there asking questions. If Lawrence followed his past record, he'd come home and knock Nita around a bit, blaming her for the fact that the police were on to his protection racket.

Gabe's knuckles were white where he gripped the steering wheel, imagining that it was Lawrence Moodie's neck.

"You're takin' this all a little too personal, sugar," Annie said lightly.

"How else should I take it?" he snapped, throwing her a quick, angry look as he flipped on the turn signal. "We just left a nineteen-year-old girl back there with a black eye and bruises all over her arms. And Moodie is going to show up as soon as we're gone and beat the hell out of her again. And we didn't even get anything useful out of her."

He slammed his fist against the steering wheel, the motion full of barely contained frustration.

"You're a cop, Gabriel, not God. You can't make everyone's problems right, no matter how much you'd like to."

"We're supposed to be taking people like Moodie off the street," he said tightly.

"And we will, but we can't arrest him until we've got enough evidence to build a solid case against him."

"And in the meantime, he uses a nineteen-year-old girl as a punching bag."

"Like I said, she's got to make the first move. Last time I checked, kidnappin' was still illegal, even when it's for someone's own good."

"Well, I think that's a gross oversight in the legal codes," Gabe complained. But he sounded more resigned than angry.

Neither of them spoke for a few minutes. They'd been partners long enough; spent so many hours together that they were long past the need to fill the silence with conversation.

"I'm thinking about resigning," Gabe said abruptly. He glanced at Annie, judging her reaction. She looked less surprised than he felt at having actually said the words out loud.

"Have you told the captain yet?"

"No." He shot her another look, not sure whether to be annoyed or amused at her calm acceptance. Amusement seemed most appropriate. "Aren't you going to express your stunned disbelief? How much you'd like me to stay on?"

Annie's mouth curved up in a smile. "Well, I'd be lyin' if I said I hadn't seen this comin', sugar."

"Do you know how annoying it is to have spent hours agonizing over a decision only to have someone say that she knew what you were going to decide all along?''

Annie grinned at his plaintive tone. ''I know. It's one of my most irritatin' habits,'' she drawled. ''Drives Bill crazy, the way I'm always right.''

''And modest, too.''

Gabe felt his black mood dissolving. Annie was right. He couldn't make everyone's problems his personal responsibility. A job like this required the ability to distance yourself from the misery that was an inevitable part of the work. He was losing that ability.

''Have you decided to quit for sure?''

''I think so. I'm losing my perspective, Annie. I used to be able to take something like this mess with Nita in stride. You do the best you can but you can't always solve the problem. You concentrate on the ones that go right, not the ones that go wrong.'' He recited the trite maxims as if they were printed on the windshield in front of them.

''You know that's the truth, sugar. You can't beat yourself up over the ones you can't help.''

''It's getting harder and harder to believe that.''

''Then it's probably time to quit before you get yourself killed tryin' to help someone who doesn't want to be helped.''

''That's what I figured.''

Annie smoothed her fingers over the crisp crease in her slacks, her expression thoughtful.

"Does this decision have anything to do with Charity Williams?"

"Indirectly," he said at last, aware that Annie was waiting for an answer. "But I think this has been coming for a long time."

The decision to leave the force *had* been a long time coming, but Gabe had expected to have more doubts when he finally made it. Instead he was filled with relief.

He wasn't sorry he'd joined the force, and he didn't regret the years he'd spent as a cop. In his more optimistic moments, he felt he'd made a difference, at least for a few people.

But the time to leave was now, while he still felt good about the job, before—as Annie had put it—he got himself killed trying to help someone who didn't want help.

How much of the decision was because of Charity, he couldn't say. Certainly she'd influenced his thinking. All the logic in the world couldn't wipe out the guilt he felt about her. He'd played the scene over in his mind a thousand times, and he honestly couldn't see what he could have done differently, but that didn't change the fact that he'd shot her.

But it wasn't just guilt over the shooting that had made him decide to leave the force. These past few weeks he'd begun to crave something more from life. Charity was the sort of woman who made a man be-

gin to think of hearth and home, of building a life with
someone, maybe even kids.

He was more than half in love with her, he admitted to himself. Her smile, her spirit, the way she kept
fighting even when he could see the fear in her eyes—
all of those were things he admired. But it was the
moments when he saw her vulnerability that had made
his heart drop into her hands.

The anger and frustration she'd felt over the deba-
cle with the flour; the way she'd clung to him in the
pool. He'd wanted nothing more than to gather her up
in his arms and hold her close, promise that nothing
would ever hurt her again.

Annie might have suggested that it was just his
overdeveloped sense of chivalry speaking, but he
didn't think it was quite that simple. He would admit
that he had a tendency to want to fix the world's ills.
But there was more than protectiveness in his feelings
for Charity.

He cared for her. He wasn't quite ready to admit to
anything deeper at this point, but he definitely cared
for her. He was even starting to wonder whether or not
she'd be interested in living on a ranch in Wyoming.

THREE DAYS after her brother's rather explosive visit,
Charity was beginning to wonder if it had been a mistake to stay at Gabe's house. It seemed as if Gabe had
been distracted ever since.

Had she misread his signals? Only a few minutes before Brian's arrival, he'd talked her out of moving out—kissed her out of it, really. Surely he hadn't changed his mind in less than five minutes. But there was no denying that even when he was home in the same room, he didn't seem to be quite there.

Charity glowered down at her unresponsive legs. He felt guilty about the shooting—he'd admitted as much. He'd also said that the guilt was separate from wanting her. But how realistic was that?

Wasn't it more likely that he'd convinced himself that he desired her? That he was trying to make her feel better about the wheelchair. Maybe he wanted her to feel that she could live a full and active life, even if she never walked again.

God knows, he had to be wondering how likely that was. With every passing day, it was getting harder and harder to believe that her paralysis was temporary.

"What are you scowling at?" Diane's question made Charity turn her head to look at her sister. Diane was sprawled in a lounger beside the pool. Her perfect size-six body was barely clad in a deceptively simple one-piece swimsuit. Her skin gleamed with layers of sun block.

She looked like an ad for the perfect "California blonde," 1990s style, minus the deep tan that would have been de rigueur in the sixties.

Charity sighed, looking down at her own pale legs. It wasn't their pallor that bothered her. If only they'd move.

"You know, if you'd stop worrying about it so much, you'd probably walk a lot sooner," Diane said, guessing the direction of her sister's thoughts.

"Thanks for the advice," Charity snapped. "When was the last time you were paralyzed?"

"You're not paralyzed." Diane swung her legs to the ground, sitting on the edge of the lounger. Reaching up, she removed her sunglasses, fixing concerned green eyes on her younger sister. "You've got to keep thinking positive."

"I'm sick and tired of thinking positive. It hasn't done me a bit of good. And I'm really tired of hearing people who are walking around on two perfectly good legs, telling me to 'think positive.'" Her voice took on a nasty, mimicking edge as she repeated the words.

"Sorry," Diane said stiffly. "I was only trying to help." She reached down to slip on her sandals. "Maybe it's time I left."

Charity watched her shrug into a gauzy beach robe and pick up the bottle of sunscreen. Her conscience nagged at her, demanding attention no matter how hard she tried to ignore it.

"Wait." She reached out to grab Diane's arm before the other woman stood up. Diane waited, her expression stiff.

"I'm the one who's sorry," Charity said. She sighed. "I seem to have developed a temper like a rabid wolf lately. I shouldn't have snapped at you like that."

She felt Diane's arm relax beneath her finger an instant before she gave the smile that had graced countless magazine covers.

"That's okay. I shouldn't spout trite phrases at you."

"Trite phrases are about all anyone can offer at this point. No." She held up her hand. "Don't tell me that I've got to keep believing I'll walk again. I *do* believe it. Sort of. Most of the time."

"Well, I believe it completely, all the time," Diane said fiercely.

"Thanks. It helps to know somebody does." She sighed again, her hand dropping away from her sister's arm as she relaxed back in the chair. "I just get so impatient," she said, half to herself.

"Of course you do. But you've got to use that impatience, make it work for you." She caught the look Charity sent her and broke off with a laugh. "Okay, so I sound like a book of maxims for salesmen. But it's true and you know it."

"I guess."

Charity was aware of Diane's concern and she tried to project a more positive attitude. She didn't know why it had gotten so difficult to maintain that image lately. A combination of Gabe's distraction and her own building frustration, maybe. Whatever it was, it wasn't Diane's fault, and she didn't want her sister to worry any more than she already did.

"You know what you need?" Diane spoke so suddenly that Charity started.

"What?" *Besides legs that worked?*

"You need to get out of this house. You haven't set foot off this lot since you got out of the hospital, except to go back to the hospital. No wonder you're feeling gloomy."

"I don't think so." Charity's hands locked on the arms of the chair.

"Of course you don't think so." Diane pursued the idea with ruthless good cheer. "You've gotten used to being here, and it feels nice and safe. But you should get out, see some new faces."

"And watch them stare at my legs?" Charity interrupted, not caring if she was being rude. Just the thought of going out in public was enough to make her sick to her stomach.

"No one's going to stare at your legs, Char."

"Oh, come on." Charity rolled her eyes, swallowing the urge to scream a refusal. "You don't believe that any more than I do. Maybe no one would be rude enough to gawk, but they'd steal little glances at me, wondering what's wrong with me, wondering if it's something marvelously interesting and fatal."

"I think you're underestimating people, Char."

"No, I'm not. I'm not saying anyone would be un-
kind. Or that they wouldn't feel sorry for me. But it's
only human to wonder about something like this." She
thumped the chair for emphasis. "I've been on the
other side, remember? You see someone with a
handicap and you wonder. You pity. And you thank
heavens it isn't you."

Diane was silenced by the bitter accuracy of her
words. But she wasn't quite ready to give up on getting Charity out for a little while.

"We wouldn't have to go where there were a lot of
people. A restaurant, maybe, at off hours. Or even
just a park."

"No. If I was going to be in this thing permanently,
you'd be right. It would be important for me to learn
to cope with the limitations of the wheelchair. But I'm
not going to be like this permanently. I'm not."

There was steely determination in her voice. Diane's suggestion had renewed her determination to get
back the use of her legs. It was all a matter of willpower and work. She was willing to put in any amount
of work, and her willpower had simply needed a small
boost. Diane had unwittingly given her that.

IT WAS stubborn determination not to lose even a day's
work that led her to get in the pool alone the next day.
The physical therapist had called to say she was going
to be an hour late. Even that small delay was intoler-
able to Charity in her current mood.

As far as she could determine, the exercises had had no effect, but the doctors and the therapist kept telling her how important it was to maintain her muscle tone.

After assuring Mary that she wasn't upset by the delay, Charity wheeled herself out to the pool and stared at the blue water, feeling frustration building inside. It was ridiculous to think that an hour's delay in her therapy session was going to make a bit of difference. But it didn't feel like an hour. It felt like a week.

Of course, she supposed she could ask Gabe to help her. It was his day off. He'd been shut in the den all day, but she didn't doubt that he'd drop whatever he was doing to help her with her exercises. Probably hoping to get her off his hands a little quicker, she thought gloomily.

Heaven knows, since that rather steamy kiss in the kitchen, he'd hardly seemed to know who she was. No. That wasn't really fair. He certainly didn't ignore her or treat her with any less courtesy than he had before Brian's noisy visit. He just didn't seem terrifically focused at the moment.

"And it probably has absolutely nothing to do with you," she told herself firmly, her voice barely audible. "Don't be such a paranoid egotist."

No doubt Gabe had any number of things on his mind besides her. It was silly to think that his every mood reflected something to do with her.

It wasn't only his odd mood that made her reluctant to ask him to help her with her exercises. Vivid in her memory was the first, last and only time he'd helped her. And it wasn't the fear she'd felt when she went under the water that she thought of first. It was the feel of Gabe's water-cooled skin under her palms, the heat of his mouth on hers. Just remembering made her skin tingle.

No, she wasn't going to ask Gabe to help her. Which meant she was just going to have to wait until Mary got here. Waiting an hour wouldn't kill her, even if it felt like it would.

Of course, she could go in the pool alone. There wasn't much she could do, but there were one or two exercises that she might be able to manage. Besides, it would be nice and cool in the water.

She glanced up at the pale blue sky. The temperature was hovering near ninety and the water looked awfully inviting. Her eyes fell on the bright orange life vest that she'd been wearing since the session with Gabe where she'd gotten such a fright. With the vest on, she wouldn't be in any danger.

She looked over her shoulder at the house, feeling like a teenager about to light up a forbidden cigarette. The den was on the other side of the house, which meant Gabe couldn't even see the pool if he happened to look out a window.

Not that it was any of Gabe's business, she told herself firmly. It wasn't as if she was thinking about doing anything dangerous.

Charity reached down to scoop the lightweight life vest off the concrete. The fabric was hot under her fingers. She struggled into it, buckling it firmly in place.

One thing she'd realized in the past couple of days was that she'd been letting other people take care of her ever since the shooting. She'd completely abdicated responsibility for her life and let them make decisions for her. If it wasn't Diane, it was Gabe or the doctors or the therapist.

She set her jaw and the brake on the chair. Reaching down, she grasped first one ankle and then the other, lifting each foot off the footrest and flipping the rests up out of the way. She slid forward until she was sitting on the edge of the chair. Then she moved each leg outward until her feet hung over the water.

Sitting there, her feet hanging in thin air, she was suddenly sure that this was the stupidest thing she'd ever done in her entire life. Before she could change her mind, she used her hands to launch herself out of the chair.

It was undoubtedly the clumsiest entry anyone had ever made into a pool. She hit her legs on the edge, something she was only able to tell because the impact jarred her whole body. She landed face first in the water, feeling a moment of panic. But the life vest bobbed her upright immediately.

What if she'd injured herself when she hit the side of the pool? She wouldn't even know if she'd cut her legs. She twisted, trying to get a look at the backs of her legs but it was beyond her.

Swiping her wet hair out of her face, she told herself to stay calm. At worst she might have scraped the skin a little. But she could hardly have gashed herself to the bone on the concrete pool edging. Besides, at least she wouldn't have to worry about sharks.

The thought made her giggle and she clapped a hand over her mouth, wondering if she was about to become hysterical. But she didn't feel hysterical. Now that the initial fright had passed, she actually felt rather proud of herself.

Dropping her hand back into the water, she laughed aloud. Stretching her arms out, she waved her hands back and forth, turning a full circle in the pool. The water felt wonderful, a cool contrast to the blazing hot sun. As always, the buoyancy of the water helped compensate for the lack of feeling in her legs. It was almost possible to pretend that there was nothing wrong with them.

She tilted her head back, closing her eyes against the sun, savoring the feel of it on her face. There was no real point in pretending that she'd really believed she could do any of her exercises by herself. The real point had been to prove that she could do something on her own, even if it was something as foolish and essentially purposeless as getting into the pool alone.

Charity floated, letting all the tension drain out of her. With her eyes closed, she could imagine herself floating in some exotic island lagoon. Any minute, a gorgeous man, wearing nothing but a pair of minuscule briefs would walk out of the jungle. He'd be tall with green-gold eyes and unruly sun-streaked brown hair. He'd smile at her and—

"What the hell do you think you're doing!"

The dream popped like a bubble pierced by a pin. Charity had been half drowsing, but Gabe's angry voice was better than a fire siren for banishing any lingering sleepiness.

Lifting one hand to shade her eyes against the sun, she peered up at him. He stood on the edge of the pool, his hands on his hips, glaring down at her. Though his face was shadowed, she didn't need to see his expression to know that his mood was less than light. His body language was perfectly clear.

He was absolutely furious.

Chapter Twelve

"Excuse me?" She hadn't done anything wrong, she reminded herself. But it was a little hard to keep in mind when he stood there glowering down at her.

"You heard me. What the hell are you doing?"

Charity lifted her chin. She didn't particularly care for his tone.

"I'm relaxing in the pool," she said, making it clear that she thought that should have been obvious.

"Alone?"

"Unless there's someone here I hadn't noticed."

"Are you crazy?"

"I don't think so," she said stiffly.

"Well, you couldn't prove it by me."

"I don't recall asking you. What are you doing?"

He was wearing black running shorts and a dark gold polo shirt. Now he was stripping the shirt off over his head, tossing it onto the concrete.

"You're getting out," he said flatly.

"I'm not sure I want to get out," she protested.

"Tough."

He jumped into the water. The waves from his entry into the pool reached her just before he did. Charity had been prepared to protest his macho treatment but she swallowed the words when she got a good look at his face.

She'd never seen Gabe so angry. His jaw was set like granite. His eyes met hers for only an instant, but Charity felt singed by that brief look.

The water lapped around Gabe's collarbone as he stopped beside her. She expected him to take her by the arm and tow her to the side of the pool.

Once she was out of the water, she was going to explain calmly and coolly that she didn't care for his overbearing attitude. She would make it clear that just because she was staying in his house, he didn't have the right to treat her like a child. She would make him understand—

"Oh!" Gabe scooped her up in his arms and strode to the steps. Charity's arms circled his neck automatically. He carried her as easily as if she were a child, striding up the steps and onto the concrete decking.

"Put me down." She bit her lip in annoyance. She sounded like the heroine in a grade B movie. But she didn't like being so close to him. It was hard to remember how angry she was when she could feel the steady thumping of his heart against her breast.

"Gladly." But he didn't put her into her wheelchair. He set her on the redwood lounger. "Now, would you like to explain what you thought you were doing?''

"I don't think so.'' She dragged the tattered remnants of her dignity around her. ''I don't see why you're so upset.''

"Oh, you don't?'' It was obvious that his brief foray into the water hadn't cooled his temper by even a degree.

"No, I don't,'' she snapped. ''I was wearing a life vest.'' She wrenched at the buckles of it as she spoke, tossing it onto the decking. She glared up at Gabe, furious that he'd spoiled her small triumph. ''There was nothing to worry about.''

"I had no way of knowing that.'' He stood over her, dripping wet, his anger so palpable that she wouldn't have been surprised to see the water turn to pure steam on his skin.

"Why would you think anything else?''

"I looked out the window, expecting to see you waiting for Mary. Instead, I see that—'' He thrust an accusing finger to where her wheelchair lay next to the pool. Her precipitous exit from it had tipped it onto its side.

Charity stared at it, realizing how it must have looked. From the house he couldn't have seen her in the water. All he would have seen was the overturned chair.

Illogically her anger didn't abate with the realization that he'd had reason to be worried. It had seemed such a simple thing. All she'd wanted was to do something—however minor—to exercise some tiny amount of control over her life.

She hadn't meant to worry Gabe. And what had he been doing looking out the window, anyway?

"I thought you'd fallen into the pool," he said.

"Well, I didn't," she snapped. She blinked back tears of frustration.

"I didn't know that. You could have drowned." He raised his voice on the last, as if she might not have grasped the possibilities.

"Maybe that would be a relief," Charity all but shouted, frustration bubbling up inside her.

"Don't say that." Gabe sank to his knees on the decking beside the chair. "Don't ever say that."

"Maybe it's the way I feel," she muttered without looking at him.

She hadn't realized the tears had escaped until his hand came up to brush them away. She batted his fingers aside.

"Go away."

"Hush." The sight of her tears seemed to have washed away his anger.

"Just go away," she said, trying to turn her face away. "I'm sorry you were worried. Now leave me alone."

"I wasn't worried. I was scared to death." He cupped one hand around her chin, tilting her face to his, brushing her tears away with his other hand.

"Don't be nice to me," she mumbled, feeling like a fool. If he was too nice, she was likely to burst into tears and make a total fool of herself.

"Would you rather I was mean?" Gentle amusement laced the words.

"Yes." She sighed, blinking back the tears. "It would be easier to take. I'm sorry I scared you."

"I'm sorry I yelled at you." His thumb brushed across her lips.

"I just wanted to feel like I was doing something on my own. Like I was in control of my life again." She looked into his eyes, trying to see if he understood what she was saying.

"Next time, warn me, would you?"

Warn him of what? she wondered dazedly. Was it possible to drown in someone's eyes?

His thumb brushed across her mouth again, and her lips parted, as if in answer to a silent command. Gabe's eyes dropped to her mouth for an instant before sweeping back up to hers. His gaze was more gold than green. She closed her eyes, unable to sustain the intensity of his look.

She felt his breath brush across her mouth an instant before his lips touched hers. Her breath left her on a sigh, her hands moving up to clutch his bare shoulders.

It was just as it had been before. Passion flared between them. Rising in a quick, stunning tide that swept her along.

His mouth slanted fiercely over hers, his tongue sliding past the barrier of her teeth to twine over hers. Charity welcomed the sensuous touch. Her fingers buried themselves in the damp hair at the back of his neck, drawing him closer.

Gabe groaned deep in his throat, his arms lifting her further onto the lounge, his lean body following her, half pressing her into the cushions.

Charity murmured a protest as his mouth left hers, but it turned to a sigh of pleasure as his tongue found the delicate curve of her ear. She arched her neck to allow him better access as he dragged his mouth the length of her throat, finding and testing the pulse that beat frantically at its base.

One strong hand cupped the back of her head. The hand that had been resting against her waist slid upward and Charity's breath caught when he boldly cupped her breast. She stiffened, only to melt when his thumb brushed across the taut peak of her nipple.

Her fingers tightened in his hair, dragging his mouth back up to hers, and she heard Gabe's rumble of approval as their lips met.

She'd never felt this kind of frantic need before. Her whole body seemed to pulse with it. The sun that blazed down from the sky was surely no hotter than the heat they were generating between the two of them.

Her hands slid over his sun-warmed back, feeling the muscles rippling under her fingers. She wanted him, needed him in a way she'd never needed anything before. It was as if he was a part of her, missing all her life and finally back where he belonged.

His hand left her breast, sliding along the indentation of her waist, pausing there, savoring the feel of her yielding beneath him. Charity thought she could never get enough of him, never give enough in return.

His hand slid lower, his thumb brushing over her hip bone before stroking downward.

"No!" Hands that a moment before had been holding him close were suddenly frantically pushing him away.

"What the . . ." Gabe's head jerked up, his eyes still dark gold with hunger.

"Don't." The choked word was all she could get out, her hands still pushing against his shoulders.

"Don't?" He shook his head, trying to clear his mind of lingering passion. "Don't what?"

"Let me go," she ordered tightly.

"What's wrong?" He still couldn't quite absorb the abrupt change in her. "Did I hurt you?"

She shook her head. "I just don't want you to touch me there."

"Where?" His brows rose as understanding came. "Your legs? You don't want me to touch your legs?"

She nodded, turning her face away. It made her feel sick even to think of him putting his hands on her legs.

"Does it hurt you?" he asked, bewildered.

"No, it doesn't hurt," she said tautly. "I can't feel anything, remember? I can't feel it when you touch me. I can't feel anything. Let me go."

"Calm down, sweetheart. There's nothing to be afraid of."

If she hadn't been so upset, she might have noticed the endearment, might have taken pleasure in his tenderness. But all she wanted was for him to go away. Something that had been so wonderful had turned to ashes.

"I don't need your pity," she told him, her voice climbing.

"Who said anything about pity? Did it feel like I was pitying you?"

"How would I know?" she snapped. "Go away."

"I'm not going to go away until you calm down and listen to me. I've touched your legs before when I picked you up and you didn't get upset."

"That was different." She refused to meet his eyes. "Get off me." How could she explain the difference to him when she couldn't even explain it to herself? And how was she supposed to explain anything at all when he was practically on top of her?

"Charity." He caught her chin in his hand, turning her face to his. His eyes were all golden green, warm with emotion.

"I'm falling in love with you."

Just one simple sentence, but Charity felt as if her world had been picked up and given a hard shake and when it was set down, it wouldn't ever be the same again. Her eyes widened in shock.

"No."

"Yes." Gabe's half-amused look hid the anxiety she was too upset to see.

"No. You're just saying that to make me feel better."

"I'm saying it because it's true. I'm falling in love with you."

"No!" She didn't want to hear it. She was afraid she might believe it. And when reality came crashing in, she wouldn't be able to deal with the heartbreak.

"I didn't mean to upset you," Gabe said, easing away from her.

"I'm not upset. And I wish you'd stop saying that," she added on a frantic note that gave the lie to her first statement.

"Okay. But not saying it doesn't mean it's not true."

"Stop it." She pushed against his shoulders, levering herself away. "You don't love me. You just think you should." She pushed again, wanting him to be gone, wanting to lock herself away somewhere. Somewhere where she didn't have to hear things that she desperately wanted to believe.

She was so focused on her emotional turmoil that she'd completely forgotten her physical limitations; forgotten legs that didn't move; forgotten everything beyond her desire to put some distance between herself and Gabe.

Her left leg shifted toward the edge of the lounger. It was only an inch, hardly enough to notice. But Charity noticed.

"Oh my God." Charity's nails dug into Gabe's shoulders, her eyes snapping to his, a mixture of hope and fear darkening them to a muddy green.

"What's wrong?" He picked up on her sudden tension, his expression changing from one of chagrined amusement to concern. "Are you hurt?"

"No." She swallowed, afraid to even voice the thought out loud. What if she'd imagined the small movement? What if she could never do it again?

"What is it Charity?" Gabe caught her arms, his eyes searching.

"My leg," she whispered. "I think it moved."

He stared at her as the realization of what this could mean swept over him. Joy blazed over his features.

"Can you do it again?" Neither of them noticed that he'd lowered his voice to match hers, as if speaking above a whisper could jeopardize the miracle that might have just occurred.

"I don't know." She could hardly get the words out past the nervousness clogging her throat. "I don't know."

"Try. Just relax and concentrate." It didn't strike either of them that the two commands were mutually exclusive.

"What if I can't do it again?" she got out. Tension had made her voice thin.

"You can." He sounded so absolutely confident that she felt her own confidence take a bound upward. "Just try."

"I can't look," she said, her eyes never leaving his. "You look."

"You couldn't talk me out of it." He grinned at her as if there was no doubt about the outcome of the next few seconds; as if her entire future wasn't on the line here. She wanted to hit him and she wanted to cling to him. Since she couldn't seem to get her fingers unpeeled from his shoulders, the latter course seemed easier.

"Give it a shot, Charity."

Easy for him to say. His whole life wasn't about to be decided. She closed her eyes, too nervous to even think of offering up a prayer. It was a simple thing, really. She'd been moving her legs all her life without giving it a thought.

She concentrated every fiber of her being on her left leg, on moving it. Even the merest fraction of an inch would do. Something, anything, to show that she hadn't dreamed the earlier movement, to show that there was reason to hope for the future.

Gabe was watching. Even if her leg twitched, he'd see it and tell her. But she didn't need him to tell her. She felt the movement. Not much, certainly—an inch

or less—but it didn't matter how much she moved.
Only that she'd moved her leg.

Her eyes flew open, reading the confirmation in
Gabe's eyes that she didn't really need. She stared at
him, hardly able to absorb the miracle.

"I moved." It wasn't a question but he answered it
anyway.

"You moved."

"I think I'm going to cry." She blinked moisture
from her eyes.

"No, you're not." Gabe sat up, pulling her into a
sitting position. "You'll be walking before you know
it. Next thing you know, you'll be running marathons. Hell, you'll probably be ready for the next
Olympics."

Swept along on his extravagant vision, Charity
laughed shakily. "Don't you think you're going a little overboard? I've never run a marathon in my life."

"It's never too late to start." His smile faded.
"God, Charity, this is all I've wanted since the shooting. Just to see you walk again."

"Well, I'm not walking yet." She was trying desperately to rein in her hopes. "It could have been a
fluke."

"It wasn't a fluke. I can feel it in my gut." His
hands slid down her arms to take hold of her fingers.
"This is your big break, kid," he said, in his best im-
itation of a studio mogul.

"I hope so, Gabe. God, I hope so."

"I know so." In that moment, with Gabe holding her, his eyes bright with belief, Charity didn't doubt that he was right.

IF CHARITY had been determined to keep up her exercises before, she became obsessed with them now. Given even a fragment of progress, she wasn't going to let it slip away. She spent as much time at her exercises as Mary would allow.

And she made progress. Agonizingly slow at first but it *was* progress. Every tiny step forward was a triumph, even if she promptly took two steps back.

Now that she had reason to believe she really would walk again, she focused every fraction of her energy on that goal.

The more she concentrated on regaining the use of her legs, the less time she had to think about Gabe, to think about him saying he loved her. She didn't want to think about that. If she thought about it too much, she might begin to believe it, and that would almost certainly lead to nothing but heartache.

"PLEASE, DIANE. Please say you'll come and stay." Charity was not too proud to beg. Her sanity was more important than her pride. She couldn't take much more time alone in Gabe's house. It was either convince Diane to move in or she would have to move out.

"Why? Does Gabe turn into a werewolf at midnight or something?" Diane leaned back in her chair, giving her sister a suspicious look.

"Of course not. It has nothing to do with Gabe," she lied.

"Then why do you want me to move in? And wouldn't Gabe have some objections?"

"I already asked him and he said he didn't mind." Charity shifted uneasily, remembering the way his brows had risen. Something in his eyes had told her that he knew exactly why she wanted her sister to move in and that it had nothing to do with her rather tangled explanation about Diane helping with her therapy.

It had been a thin excuse at best since Gabe knew as well as she did that Diane would be gone most of the day. So unless Charity expected to work on her therapy in the middle of the night, there wasn't much by way of practical reasons for her sister to move in.

"There's no practical reason for me to move in," Diane said bluntly.

"Can't you just do it because I asked you to," Charity suggested hopefully.

"Of course." Charity had only a moment to feel relieved at her prompt agreement before Diane continued. "But if I'm going to move to Pasadena when my home and business are in Beverly Hills I don't think it's unreasonable of me to be curious about why

I'm doing it. Not to mention that you're asking me to move next door to that dreadful prig of a doctor.''

"Jay isn't a prig," Charity said, taking on the most minor objection first.

"You couldn't prove it by me. The man looks at me like I'm an insect."

"You just don't know how to cope when a man doesn't fall panting at your feet. It's not an uncommon experience for us mere mortals."

"I don't expect a man to pant at my feet." She caught Charity's disbelieving look and shrugged. "Okay, so maybe I've gotten used to a pant or two. But there's got to be something between panting and sneering. And don't think you're going to distract me from the point of this whole conversation," she added, fixing Charity with a stern look. "*Why* do you want me to move in?"

Charity ran her fingers along the arm of her wheelchair—the wheelchair she would soon be leaving behind.

"It's Gabe, isn't it," Diane said.

"More or less." Charity sighed. She should have known she wasn't going to be able to fob Diane off with some thin story.

"What did he do?"

"He told me he was falling in love with me."

Seeing Diane's stunned expression almost made it worth having to explain. Diane blinked, opened her mouth and closed it again and then sat staring at her as if she wasn't sure she'd heard correctly.

"Well. The beast! How dare he! Shall we call the police?"

"He is the police," Charity reminded her. She smiled at Diane's exaggerated indignation.

"That doesn't mean he can say that he's falling in love with you! What kind of a fiend would do that?"

"Okay, okay. So it doesn't seem like a serious problem to you. But it is to me."

"Why?"

"Why?" The simple question stumped her for a moment.

"Yes, why? You feel the same way about him, don't you?"

"Of course not." Her denial trailed off under Diane's stern look. "That's not the point."

"You love him. He loves you. That seems to be very much the point."

"But he *doesn't* love me," Charity cried. "That's the problem. He only *thinks* he loves me. It's really just because he feels guilty about the shooting. If it hadn't been for that, he'd never have noticed me at all."

"Why are you so sure that's all it is? You're a terrific person. Why is it so hard to believe Gabe could really be in love with you?"

Charity ran her hands restlessly over the wheels of the chair. She didn't want to hear what Diane was saying. There was nothing she'd like more to believe than that Gabe was in love with her. But all her instincts were telling her that she was going to get hurt if she didn't keep all the facts clearly in mind.

The fact was that Gabe felt guilty about her paralysis. It wouldn't have been hard to confuse some of that guilt with something that seemed like love.

"I just don't want to be here alone with him," she said finally, sidestepping Diane's question. "Will you come and stay?"

"Of course I will, Char. If it means that much to you, you know I will. But I'm going on record as saying that you're going to regret it if you walk away from this without at least giving it a chance. Gabe is a great guy and he's had the good taste to fall in love with you. Don't let him get away."

Charity nodded. It was easier to pretend to agree with Diane than to argue. As for Gabe's feelings for her, she was going to try not to think about that until she could walk. Once she was walking again, she'd see if Gabe still thought he loved her.

Chapter Thirteen

Charity sank into the wheelchair with a bump. Her face was shiny with sweat, her arms ached from the effort of holding herself upright on the parallel bars, and her legs felt like overcooked spaghetti. But she was grinning from ear to ear. She tilted her head back to look at Diane, seeing the happy tears in her sister's eyes.

"Not bad, huh?"

"Not bad?" Diane's voice shook with emotion. "You were fantastic! I can't wait to tell Brian."

"Maybe once he hears this, he'll stop treating Gabe like a serial killer," Charity said. She wiped her face with the towel draped around her neck.

"Gabe is going to be so thrilled."

"I'm not going to tell him. Not yet."

Diane's eyes narrowed on her sister. "Why not? I know you've got some doubts about your relationship but he'll be so thrilled about this."

"I know. But it isn't like I'm *really* walking yet."

"But you're making so much progress."

"I'll tell him," Charity said. "I just want to do it in my own time and in my own way. Promise you won't say anything?"

Diane nodded reluctantly. "If that's what you want."

"It is."

"So YOU'VE really done it." Annie's words were half statement, half question.

"I handed in my resignation," Gabe confirmed. He leaned back in his desk chair and put his feet up on the corner of the desk, hands behind his head, as he grinned at her. "I am about to join the ranks of the unemployed."

"You were just waitin' until we nailed Moodie, weren't you?" Annie leaned against the side of the desk.

"Yep."

"It meant that much to you to put him away?"

"I wouldn't have felt good about leaving him on the streets."

"Because of Nita?"

"Maybe." He lowered his hands and dropped his feet from the desk. "Maybe I just wanted to go out on a positive note. And leaving Lawrence Moodie loose would *not* have been a positive note."

Annie eased one hip onto the corner of the desk. She tilted her head to one side, studying him. Gabe raised his brows. "Do I have a smut on my nose? Or are you just trying to memorize my face so you won't miss me so much when I'm gone?"

"I'm just tryin' to remember when I've seen you so relaxed. I think the last time was at Jim Briggs's weddin' when you drank half a bowl of punch and serenaded us all with your version of 'Tangerine.'"

"If you're implying that I had consumed more liquor than I could hold with dignity, I deny the charge," he said stiffly.

"Dignity? You and dignity weren't even kissin' cousins that night, sugar." She dodged the wad of paper he threw at her, grinning. "You certainly proved you weren't the next Perry Como."

"You know, the real question isn't why I'm resigning," Gabe suggested. "The real question is how I managed to live with you as a partner all these years."

"Just lucky, I guess." They grinned at each other, in perfect accord.

Annie's smile was the first to fade. "You know, I am goin' to miss you. This place just won't be the same without you around to annoy me."

"Maybe you'll be lucky and your next partner will be just as irritating," Gabe suggested.

"Impossible."

Gabe glanced around the station house. Already he felt a certain distance from it. A good percentage of his life had been spent here—some of it good, some of it bad—and he was going to miss it. But it was time to move on. And he didn't think he'd be looking over his shoulder, wishing he'd made a different choice.

"You goin' to join your dad and become a cow-poke?" Annie asked, breaking the slightly melancholy silence that had fallen between them.

"I've been giving it some thought. Wide-open spaces have a certain appeal after L.A."

"You takin' Charity with you?"

Gabe shot her a sharp look, not at all fooled by her casual tone. Annie had been worried about his involvement with Charity from the beginning. She thought he was going to take a nasty fall. She could be right, he acknowledged ruefully, thinking of the distance Charity kept between them these days.

"If she'll go," he admitted slowly.

"And if she won't? Would you still go?"

"Well, that would depend on why she wouldn't go." He picked up a pencil and turned it idly between his fingers. "If she isn't too fond of Wyoming, we could work something else out. If she isn't too fond of me, then I guess there wouldn't be much reason to hang around, would there?"

"Any woman in her right mind would be glad to move anywhere with you," Annie said loyally.

"Thanks. Now if I could just be sure Charity was in her right mind."

"How's she gettin' along with learnin' to walk again and all?" Annie straightened an untidy stack of papers on his desk.

"I guess it's going pretty well." Gabe shrugged. "She doesn't discuss it with me. But I gather everyone's happy with her progress."

The truth was that Charity didn't discuss much of anything with him these days. She held Diane as a shield between them. Gabe could almost laugh at her obvious machinations to make sure they were never alone together. Almost.

"You really love her, don't you?" Annie's soft question made him realize that he'd been staring at her without really seeing her. His mouth curved in a half-embarrassed smile.

"Yeah. I really love her."

THE PROBLEM WAS how to convince Charity that he *really* did love her.

He'd never had occasion to tell a woman he loved her until now, which meant he was far from being an expert in the matter, but he hadn't expected his declaration to strike terror in Charity's heart.

That she didn't believe him was obvious. She was sure his feelings were more guilt than love. And for some reason he couldn't begin to fathom, she had the odd notion that she wasn't the type of woman he could love. It was funny, really. He'd never thought of himself as having a particular "type." Of course, now that he'd gotten to know Charity, it was perfectly obvious that she was his "type."

What wasn't so obvious was how she felt about him. There'd been moments when he was almost sure she loved him. But the rest of the time he wondered if he was just imagining that she felt the same way.

Give her time, he told himself, reining in his impatience. The past few weeks had been rough on her, to put it mildly. She'd been shot, lost her ability to walk and most of her independence. No wonder she wasn't ready to jump into a relationship. He'd wait until she was walking again before pressing the issue.

Once she was walking again, he'd be able to convince her that his feelings went far deeper than guilt. And once she understood how much he loved her... Well, he had to trust to fate for anything beyond that.

He just had to be patient.

GABE REPEATED that promise all the way home. Having made the commitment to leave the force, he wanted to run in the door, sweep Charity up in his arms and ask her what she thought of living in Wyoming. But that would be a less-than-prudent course of action, he reminded himself.

He flipped on the turn signal and eased the battered old Jag onto the off ramp. She felt something for him. She wouldn't have responded the way she had when he kissed her if she hadn't felt something. He just had to give her some time and a little space.

He'd worked late, and despite the extra hours of daylight that summer brought, it was nearly dark by the time he turned onto his street. He pulled the Jag into the drive and flicked off the engine but he didn't get out immediately. Rolling his head, he tried to ease the ache in his neck from too many hours of paperwork.

Then he sat and stared at the lights in the house as if he might find answers in their soft glow. If he could just be sure that Charity loved him, the waiting wouldn't be so difficult.

Sighing, he pushed open the car door and eased his long legs out of the low-slung car. He wasn't getting any closer to knowing her feelings by sitting in the driveway. As he shut the Jag's door, it suddenly occurred to him that Diane's compact wasn't in the drive. Nor was it parked in the street. Which meant that, chances were, she wasn't home.

Gabe slid his hands into the back pockets of his jeans and considered the idea. Charity had made it a point not to be alone with him since Diane moved in. He wasn't sure if she was afraid he'd kiss her again or that he'd tell her he loved her. He hadn't tried to force the issue.

Right now the most important thing was for her to get well. He wouldn't do anything to distract her from that. And if, when she learned to walk again, she chose to walk out of his life, he'd just have to accept it. Just as he'd accepted her need to use Diane as a shield to keep him at a distance.

But Diane wasn't home. Did that mean Charity had decided it was safe to let him a little closer? Or did it just mean that Diane had something else to do tonight?

He pulled his hands from his pockets. He wasn't going to find out anything by standing here staring at his house.

THE MINUTE Charity heard Gabe's car in the driveway, her stomach tightened. She reached up to pat her hair. Diane had twisted it into a smooth French braid at the back of her head, leaving a few tendrils loose to frame her face.

She bit her lip. Didn't most men prefer women with their hair down? Maybe the French braid was too severe. What if Gabe thought it looked overdone? She lifted her hands, on the verge of pulling the careful braid apart.

She curled her fingers into her palms, forcing herself to lower her hands. Her hair was fine. Gabe wasn't going to worry about her hairstyle. He probably didn't know a French braid from a French fry.

What was he doing out there? Had she imagined hearing his car? God knows she was nervous enough to imagine almost anything. Moving to a mirror, she checked to make sure her makeup was okay. She'd checked it less than ten minutes ago but it never hurt to be sure. She certainly didn't want to greet him with mascara smeared under her eyes or her lipstick on crooked.

She'd chewed most of the lipstick off, actually, and her fingers were trembling too much for her to risk putting on a fresh layer. Well, at least chewing her lips had given them some color.

She turned away from the mirror, smoothing her hands over the skirt of her jade-green dress. The dress had been a present from her sister. Diane's own style might lean toward the flamboyant but she knew Charity's taste was a little more traditional. Charity had fallen in love with it the moment Diane pulled it out of the box.

The bodice was a simple cut, sleeveless with a neckline that allowed a tantalizing glimpse of the upper curves of her breasts. The waist was nipped in with a matching narrow belt. From there the skirt fell in extravagantly gathered folds to just below her knees.

It was the sort of dress that never went out of style and never looked dated. Exactly the dress to wear on a night when your confidence needs every boost it could get, she told herself. She just wished her confidence felt a little more boosted.

Where was he? She glanced at the front windows, nibbling on her lower lip. Should she look and see if she'd really heard him pull in? But what if he was out there and saw her peering out the window? She'd planned this evening too carefully to spoil it just because she was impatient.

She knew exactly how she wanted him to see her when he walked in the door. Poised and confident, standing on her own two feet. She looked down at the feet in question, wiggling her toes inside her soft flats.

She didn't think she'd ever be blasé about seeing her feet planted firmly on the floor again. It was a miracle—a miracle that she'd paid for with sweat and pain and more than a few tears. Except for that first movement, every inch of progress had been fought for. But when she'd taken her first trembling step, all the agony had suddenly seemed a small price to pay.

One of the hardest parts had been not telling Gabe every detail of her progress. She knew how much her recovery meant to him, and she'd wanted to share every step of it with him.

But she was already too close to him. Charity simply didn't have the confidence Diane did that Gabe's feelings for her would survive much past her regaining the use of her legs.

Not that she expected him to throw her out of his life the minute she could walk again. It would be more gradual than that—a slow drawing-away as he realized how much of his feelings had been guilt rather than passion.

She'd accepted that that was the way it was going to be, but she'd promised herself tonight. She pressed her hand over her stomach, trying to subdue the butterflies there.

Tonight was her last night in Gabe's house, and she knew exactly how she wanted it to go. She hadn't even told Diane what she had in mind. As far as Diane knew, she just wanted a nice, romantic dinner with Gabe. She hadn't told her sister she was leaving before morning. Let Diane argue with her when Charity turned up on her doorstep tomorrow morning.

She sighed, knowing Diane was going to think she was an idiot. But really, what was so wrong with doing it this way? Better to leave now before Gabe had to ask her to go.

And if she was wrong and he really did love her? Well, it wasn't as if she was going to refuse to see him. She was moving out, not going into hiding.

Just when she'd convinced herself that she'd imagined the sound of his car, Charity heard Gabe's key in the lock. Immediately she felt almost sick with nerves. She didn't need to look in the mirror again to know she'd paled.

She'd planned this but now that the moment had arrived, all she wanted was to beat a quick retreat. She could go and hide in her bedroom. If Gabe knocked, she could tell him she was sick—something simple and believable like the plague, maybe.

But she'd never get away before the door opened, and she did not intend his first glimpse of her on her own two feet to be her back as she scuttled out of sight. She drew a quick breath and straightened her shoulders. She leaned unobtrusively against a small side table. From the way her knees were shaking, she had some doubt about their ability to continue supporting her.

Gabe pushed open the door and stepped into the hallway. Charity heard the door click shut behind him, and her fingers tightened over the edge of the table. Maybe it hadn't been a good idea to greet him standing up. She'd wanted to show him that she was completely recovered, that there was no need for him to feel guilty anymore. But it wouldn't do much to convince him if she collapsed into a heap on the carpet.

She stiffened her knees and drew in a deep breath as she heard Gabe's footsteps crossing the foyer.

His attention was caught first by the beautifully set table. Jay and Diane had manhandled the kitchen table to its current position next to the wide back windows. They'd argued about everything from who should take which end of the table to how to get it through the doorway, but the positioning was worth listening to them.

Looking out over the backyard, with only the soft glow from the pool lights to break the darkness, it certainly had more ambience than eating in the kitchen. Diane had provided a red tablecloth, and Charity had set it with the china Gabe said had belonged to his grandmother. Two candles, as yet unlit, promised a romantic glow.

Gabe's brows rose slowly as he studied the table. The few seconds gave Charity a chance to will the strength back into her legs. His gaze left the table, shifting unerringly to where she stood across the living room.

Oddly, the first thing that struck him was that he'd never seen her looking more beautiful. The green dress made her skin look like porcelain and brought out the color of her eyes until they glowed like emeralds.

Hard on the heels of that thought was the stunning realization that she was standing. Standing. He sucked in a quick breath, feeling his heart jump in his chest. My God, she was standing! His disbelieving eyes swept over her, trying to absorb the reality of what he was seeing.

She took a step toward him, leaving the support of the small table she'd been holding. It wasn't a long step, and there was a certain stiffness in her movements that told him she didn't quite trust in the miracle.

It wasn't until she'd taken another step that the reality of it hit. He felt joy well up inside him, his chest aching with the force of it.

Charity stopped, uncertain in the face of his silence. Why didn't he say something? Do something?

"You're walking." The words taut, as if they couldn't begin to express what he wanted to say.

"Yes."

"How long?"

"A while." She linked her fingers together in front of her. Was he going to be upset that she hadn't told him sooner? "I wanted to surprise you."

"You certainly did that." There was nothing to be read from his tone, and she wondered again if she'd made a big mistake in presenting it to him this way. He moved toward her.

Charity waited. She couldn't have taken another step if her life depended on it. She felt as if she were frozen in place.

Gabe stopped in front of her, but she couldn't seem to lift her eyes from the wedge of skin left bare by his open collar. Was he furious with her? Did he think she'd kept the extent of her progress from him in an effort to keep him feeling guilty? Until this moment, it hadn't even occurred to her that it could look that way.

"Gabe, I—"

"You're walking," he said again, as if confirming it to himself. Something in his tone brought her eyes to his face, and she forgot the tangled apology she'd been going to offer. His eyes blazed with happiness— a green-gold fire that washed over her, driving out any doubts she'd had about his feelings.

He caught her hands in his, holding them out away from her sides as he looked down at her. His blatant pleasure made it impossible to feel self-conscious.

"I can't believe it. You're walking."

His grin was infectious and Charity felt her own mouth curve upward. How could she have thought, even for a moment, that he'd be concerned with anything more than that she was walking again? The one thing she'd never doubted was that Gabe wanted, with all his heart, to see her back on her feet again.

"I'm not running marathons yet."

"It's only a matter of time." He released her hands but only to grasp her by the shoulders. "You're walking."

He couldn't seem to quite grasp the miracle, even with her standing right in front of him.

"What do the doctors say? The therapist?"

"They're delighted with my progress. I'm not quite up to speed yet but everyone is sure it's just a matter of time."

"Are *you* sure it's a matter of time?" he asked, remembering the doubts she'd had about making a recovery.

"Yes." She gave a shaky laugh. "I guess walking at all seems like such a miracle that I've just accepted that I'm going to make it all the way. In a few weeks all this will seem like a dream."

"A dream." He repeated her words, wondering if she planned on him being a part of that half-forgotten dream or a part of her future. But this wasn't the time to worry about that.

"I can't seem to grasp that you're standing here. Standing!" He ran his hands up and down her bare arms as if to reassure himself that she wasn't a figment of his imagination. He grinned down at her. "You look stunning."

"Because I'm standing?" she asked, surprised by the almost flirtatious tone of the question. Diane was the Williams sister who flirted, certainly not quiet Charity. But she didn't feel like quiet Charity tonight.

Gabe's eyes widened slightly, as if he was surprised by the question. Awareness flared to life in his gaze, followed by a warmth that made Charity's skin feel hot.

"The fact that you're standing only enhances your loveliness." There was just enough playfulness in his tone to keep the compliment from sounding exaggerated.

Charity flushed, feeling the warmth spread from her cheeks, down her throat, settling in the pit of her stomach.

"Flattery will get you an extra serving of chocolate mousse pie," she suggested.

"Chocolate mousse pie?" Gabe's eyes flicked over the beautifully arranged table—set for two, he noticed. "Where's Diane?"

"You're never going to believe it, but she and Jay went out to dinner. Together."

"The airhead and the prig?" Gabe's brows rose, expressing his amazement.

"I nearly fell over in a faint. I think they're secretly attracted to each other."

"Like gunpowder and matches," Gabe muttered. To be honest, he didn't really care if Diane and Jay tore each other to pieces. He and Charity were alone, and the walls she'd so carefully erected to keep him at a distance had vanished without a trace. For the moment he couldn't ask for anything more.

"Are you hungry?" Charity's question brought his attention back to her. He wondered if she realized his hands were still on her shoulders. Her skin felt as soft as it looked. Hungry? Yes, but food wasn't the first thing that came to mind.

"Starved," he said with a smile. It took a conscious effort to release her. "Do I have time to change?"

"Yes. I'll set dinner out."

"Do you need help?"

"No, thanks."

"You won't try to lift anything too heavy?" He hesitated, clearly doubtful about the idea of leaving her on her own.

"I cross my heart," she promised solemnly.

"If you need anything, yell."

BUT CHARITY didn't need to yell. Diane had prepared everything before she left with Jay—not on a date, she'd said plainly. All Charity had to do was warm the casserole, a delicate mixture of chicken, rice and herbs, and steam the fresh broccoli. Tossed salads and a chocolate mousse pie Diane had brought from an exclusive Beverly Hills bakery completed the menu.

It wasn't exactly Wolfgang Puck, but it was tasty and simple enough that it didn't tax either her strength or her concentration.

Gabe certainly had no complaints. He'd changed into a pair of tailored black trousers that molded his muscular thighs in a positively sinful fashion and a loose dark gold shirt that made his eyes more gold than green.

He looked devastatingly attractive, and Charity found it hard to concentrate on her meal with him sitting across the small table from her. Though Gabe made a show of eating, she had the feeling that he wasn't tasting the food any more than she was.

Now that the miracle of her being able to walk had sunk in, Gabe was beginning to wonder what this was going to mean. Certainly there was no reason for her to continue to live in his house. No reason aside from the fact that he was crazy in love with her.

Would she have gone to all this trouble if she didn't feel something for him? The dress, the dinner, making sure they were alone for the first time in ages—it was all setting the stage. But for what?

Was she going to tell him she loved him? Or was she going to tell him thanks for the place to stay and so long?

Just because she moved out, it didn't mean that he was losing her forever, he reminded himself. Unless she told him never to darken her door again, there was no reason he couldn't see her. They could go out, date, spend time together in a more normal fashion. Heaven knew, there hadn't been anything particularly normal about their relationship up until now.

AFTER THE MEAL Gabe poured coffee while she carried the dessert plates out to the living room. He followed her, surprised when she bypassed the table in favor of the thickly upholstered sofa. He set the cups on the coffee table before sinking down beside her.

"You know, I always wondered what this sofa felt like," she commented as she handed him his plate. "It looked so decadent."

"Does it live up to your expectations?" he asked, trying to read her mood. Why did he get the feeling she had more than the sofa on her mind?

"Yes." Charity took a bite of pie, wondering if when she'd regained the use of her legs, she'd lost a portion of her mind.

She'd had the evening all mapped out. There was nothing unpremeditated about it. So far everything had gone according to plan. Gabe had been thrilled to see her walking. They'd shared a lovely meal. The conversation had flowed comfortably between them, even though half the time she'd had a hard time remembering what they were talking about.

Now all that was left was the final stage of the plan. The problem was she'd never in her life tried to se-

duce a man, and she wasn't at all sure how to go about
it. Even worse, she was beginning to have doubts
about the advisability of doing it at all.

Just how did one go about making it clear that one
was shamelessly eager to share a man's bed?

"The pie was marvelous," Gabe said, setting his
empty plate on the coffee table. Charity stared down
at her own plate, wondering when she'd finished her
slice of pie.

"Yes, it was good." She set her plate down and
drew in a slow breath. She was behaving like an idiot.
This was the nineties. There was nothing wrong with
a woman expressing her attraction to a man.

"You look like you're on your way to take a particularly nasty midterm," Gabe said.

She flushed, her confidence in her seduction skills
sinking to a new low. "I was just thinking that I didn't
want any coffee after all," she offered weakly. "Too
much caffeine."

"Tired?" Gabe asked. He reached out one arm and
pulled her close. Charity went willingly, laying her
head on his shoulder. It felt wonderful to be held close
to him.

"Not really," she murmured, resting her hand on
his chest. No, *tired* wasn't what she felt at all. She
toyed with the buttons on his shirt. Gabe stiffened as
she slid the first button through the buttonhole.
Keeping her cheek pressed to his shoulder, she slipped

a second one loose. But his hand closed over hers when she reached for the third button.

"You could get in trouble that way," he said softly. But there was a huskiness in his voice that told her he meant just the sort of trouble she rather hoped to get into.

"I could?" She slid the button open. Her fingers rested on bare skin now. She could feel his heart beating strong and steady. A little too fast maybe?

"Charity?" Gabe's finger cupped her chin, tilting her face up until he could see her eyes.

Her color was high but she met his gaze steadily, and he felt his pulse accelerate in a way that had nothing to do with the caffeine in the two swallows of coffee he'd had.

Only a blind man could miss the invitation in her eyes. And even a blind man could read the way her fingers moved restlessly against his chest. He wanted nothing more than to accept that invitation.

How many nights had he lain awake, thinking about her being just across the hall, wondering what it would feel like to have her in his bed, her hair spread across his pillow like honey-colored silk.

But he wanted more than just a night with her. He wanted a lifetime. Seduction had been the furthest thing from his mind tonight. Okay, maybe not the *furthest* but it certainly hadn't been part of his plans.

On the other hand, her mouth looked incredibly soft. It couldn't hurt to kiss her. Just once, he promised himself.

Her lips parted under his, and Gabe forgot all about limiting himself to one kiss. It wasn't possible to kiss her just once. Not when her mouth felt made just for him. Not when her body was so soft and yielding in his arms.

Their tongues touched and withdrew, only to touch again. It was a delicate duel where the object wasn't to win or lose, only to give and receive pleasure.

Hardly conscious of his actions, Gabe shifted her to lie across his lap. She tilted her head back to grant his mouth better access to the length of her neck. He tasted the pulse that beat at the base of her throat. He kissed his way across her shoulder, dragging aside the narrow strap that supported her bodice as he went. It dropped over her arm, leaving her shoulder bare.

His mouth came back to hers, hungry for the taste of her. Charity buried her fingers in his hair, drawing him closer, her hunger as great as his. She murmured her approval as his hand settled on her knee, sliding slowly upward under the soft silk skirt.

She caught her breath as his fingers encountered the lacy edge of her panties. Gabe felt her sudden uncertainty. He drew his head back, his palm flattening against her thigh.

Her eyes were a smoky green, dark with emotion. And desire. It took a considerable effort of will not to put his mouth to hers again and forget about everything but satisfying the hunger that had been gnawing at him for weeks.

But he wanted so much more than that from Charity. He wanted her in his bed but not just for the night. He wanted her to understand that this was more for him than a quick toss in the hay. So much more.

"Charity, I—"

"Shh." She put her fingers over his mouth, locking the words inside him. "No talk. Not tonight."

Gabe hesitated, his eyes searching hers. His instincts told him that tonight was exactly when they needed to talk. But he wasn't immune to the plea in her eyes, the invitation in her soft body.

"Later," he said softly.

"Later," she said, her agreement swallowed in the pressure of his mouth over hers.

Holding her in his arms, his mouth locked over hers, Gabe stood up from the sofa. Charity linked her hands behind his neck as he carried her into his bedroom. This was what she wanted, what she needed. And if she paid a high price for it tomorrow, it would be worth it.

Gabe set her on her feet beside the bed. His fingers moved over her hair, destroying all Diane's careful work in a matter of seconds. Charity's hair tumbled onto her shoulders in a soft honey-gold cloud. Seeing the look in his eyes, she felt truly beautiful for the first time in her life.

If she'd had any doubts about what she was doing, they were stolen away by the tenderness of Gabe's touch, the soft whisper of his voice. He explored her body with gentle thoroughness, drawing an aching response from her.

And when the time had at last come to accept him into her, Charity could no longer doubt the rightness of her choice, the absolute inevitability of this moment. This was what she'd spent a lifetime waiting for.

THIS WAS what he'd waited for all his life. Gabe felt Charity's body adjusting to him, accepting his possession. She held him as if made for only him. If he were to die at this moment, he would feel complete.

But the pleasure only built with each movement, each sigh, until at last they could climb no higher. Gabe felt the delicate contractions that took Charity, and he tumbled after her into the final moment of pleasure.

It was a long time before he gathered the strength to move and then it was only enough to ease his weight from her lax body. Her murmur of protest changed to a sigh of contentment when he slid his arm under her shoulder, pulling her against his side.

She cuddled into him, her body fitting his as if they'd been sleeping together forever. Gabe let himself drift to sleep, feeling a soul-deep contentment.

They still needed to talk, but for the first time he was confident of the outcome.

They were meant to be together. She must surely realize that now.

Chapter Fourteen

When Gabe woke the next morning, his arm swept out immediately, seeking Charity's warmth. But he was alone in the bed, the sheets cold. Frowning, he opened his eyes and glanced at the clock. It was still early, just past six-thirty.

He'd looked forward to waking with Charity in his arms. But he supposed that, after being stuck in a wheelchair all these weeks, it wasn't surprising that she wouldn't be inclined to sleep late. It must still be a novelty to be able to wake up and get out of bed.

Relaxing back into the pillow, he allowed a satisfied smile to curve his mouth. It seemed foolish now to think of how worried he'd been about the future. Obviously Charity saw it as clearly as he did. Oh, the details would still have to be worked out, but the important thing was that she loved him.

His smile faded slightly when he remembered that she'd never said as much. But she didn't have to say the words, not when she'd given so sweetly of herself.

Her love had been in her eyes, in the way she touched him.

She hadn't wanted to talk last night and maybe she'd been right. The closeness they'd shared said more than words could have. Today they'd have the words. He'd tell her that he loved her, that he'd left the force, and he'd ask her how she felt about Wyoming.

They'd talk, say all the things lovers said. And tonight he'd take her out to dinner, some elegant restaurant with a view of the city and outrageous prices.

And then they'd come home and learn all the things there hadn't been time for the night before. His smile took on a sensual edge. On the other hand, why wait until tonight?

Gabe swung his legs off the bed and lifted his robe off the back of a chair, thrusting his arms into the sleeves as he left the bedroom. He noted absently that Charity's clothes were no longer on the floor where he'd dropped them last night. He must have been sleeping like the dead to sleep through her stirring around. But then, last night was the first time he'd felt completely relaxed in a very long time.

But that feeling wasn't destined to last. It took him only a few moments to realize that the house was empty. Tightening the belt on the robe, he slid open the patio doors and walked toward the pool. The morning was already hot, promising another scorching summer day, but Gabe didn't notice the heat.

Charity wasn't in the pool and she wasn't in the house. She didn't have a car, even if she'd been up to driving it, and he doubted she'd reached that point in her recovery yet.

He strode back into the house, sliding the door shut with a snap. He was on his way into the bedroom to get dressed when he saw the note propped up on the table in front of the window. The table where they'd shared a romantic dinner the night before.

Gabe eyed the innocuous piece of paper as if it were a letter bomb. He picked it up slowly. His name was written across the front of it. He ripped it open, already sure that he wasn't going to like what it said. He was right.

Dear Gabe, I can't thank you enough for all you've done for me. Your kindness these past weeks meant a great deal to me.

His kindness! Gabe felt his temper start to simmer.

I don't want you to feel guilty about what happened. I've told you, and I meant it, that I certainly don't hold you to blame.

I hope you'll forgive my cowardice in not saying goodbye face to face. I hate goodbyes. Besides, I certainly hope we'll see each other in the future. I consider you a friend and hope you feel the same about me.

A friend? Not bloody likely. There was nothing "friendlike" about his feelings for her. And he didn't believe for a minute that she felt nothing more than friendship for him. A woman didn't respond to a friend with the kind of passion Charity had shown him last night.

I think I got all my things, but if I've forgotten anything, I'll be staying with Diane until I get a new apartment. You can contact me there.

Contact her? Right now his palm itched with the urge to make contact with her rear end.

Please don't feel as if you owe me anything because of last night. It was what I wanted.
   I'd like to think all debts are paid between us.
   Yours, Charity Williams.

Gabe curled his fingers slowly into a fist, crumpling the note into a ball. *All debts paid between them?* His blood pressure climbed another notch. Is that how she thought of last night? As if she were repaying his "kindness" to her? And signing it with her full name, as if he might not know who she was, otherwise.

Come to think of it, it was probably a good thing she'd put this drivel in a note. If she'd been standing in front of him spouting this sort of garbage, he might have strangled her with his bare hands.

All debts paid in full.

If she thought she could get rid of him that easily, she'd better think again.

Gabe tossed the crumpled note on the table and strode toward the bedroom. He had several things to say to Ms. Charity Williams.

"All debts paid in full," he muttered as he jerked open a drawer and pulled out a pair of briefs. Come to think of it, maybe he'd strangle her first and say what he had to say later.

GABE MADE record time getting from Pasadena to Beverly Hills. It was not yet eight o'clock when he stopped in front of Diane's apartment door. There was a bell but he ignored it in favor of the more satisfactory pleasure of banging his fist on the door.

Time hadn't cooled his temper. When the door wasn't answered soon enough, he knocked again, more forcefully. He was just considering kicking it in when he heard Diane's voice.

"I'm coming." She sounded annoyed. Unreasonably Gabe hoped he'd dragged her out of bed. She'd probably known about this insane plan of Charity's. That made her guilty by association, and getting her out of bed seemed a small punishment.

He glared at the peephole, hoping his expression was enough to intimidate her into opening the door.

He heard Diane mutter his name, as if answering someone's question, and then she was fumbling with the lock.

She pulled open the door, and Gabe didn't bother to wait for an invitation before stepping past her onto the thick carpeting.

"Come in," Diane murmured, but Gabe wasn't interested in sarcasm. He wasn't interested in anything but finding Charity.

His gaze swept unseeingly over an endless expanse of hopelessly impractical snow-white carpeting. The exquisite and expensive decor was lost on him.

His gaze only stumbled when it fell on a familiar figure in an unfamiliar place. Jay Baldwin stood in the hallway he assumed led to the bedrooms. He wore his pants but nothing else, and from the rumpled condition of his brown hair, it was obvious he'd just climbed out of bed.

Gabe's eyes skimmed from his neighbor to Diane, who wore a short black silk robe. From the looks of it, she'd just climbed out of the same bed as Jay. Gabe's brows rose slightly in surprise. So Charity had been right when she said they were attracted to each other.

But the distraction was momentary. He was only interested in one thing.

"Where is she?"

Diane's brows rose, her eyes snapping with interest. She studied him for a moment as if debating whether or not to answer.

"I could just kick open every door," Gabe commented to no one in particular.

"No need to go all macho on me," Diane said, grinning. "I'm on your side. I told her she was nuts."

"It's a pity she didn't listen," he growled. "Where is she?"

"Second door on the right." Diane nodded to the hallway. Gabe strode across the living room, nodding shortly to Jay as he passed. Now that he had her almost within reach, he wasn't sure whether to air his rage or kiss her until she came to her senses and admitted she loved him.

CHARITY WAS LYING on the bed in Diane's cluttered guest room, which also functioned as her workroom. She'd been staring at the ceiling to avoid staring at the incredible disarray that filled every corner of the room.

She had to start looking for a place of her own. And a job. Mr. Hoffman had promised her that she had a job with him anytime she wanted, but she couldn't imagine going back to the jewelry store. Too many memories, of the robbery as well as of Gabe. Besides, it was time she moved on, did something else with her life.

She jerked up on the bed, her breath leaving her on a startled cry as her bedroom door slammed open. Thoughts of burglars and banshees scattered when she saw Gabe's towering figure in the doorway.

The sight did nothing to still her pounding heartbeat. His expression alone was enough to make banshees look tame.

"G-Gabe," she stammered out.

"In the flesh," he said grimly.

"Wh-What are you doing here?"

"All the way over here, I've been considering the possibility of throttling you," he said, advancing into the room.

"Throttling me?" she squeaked, wondering if he'd lost his mind. "I don't understand. I left you a note." She eased back on the bed, wishing Diane hadn't piled so many boxes around the room that escape was impossible. Not that she was afraid of Gabe. At least, not really afraid.

"A note." He made the word an epithet. "It's a good thing you put that crap in a note. I'm not sure I could have held my temper if you'd said that garbage to my face."

This was holding his temper?

"I don't understand why you're so upset." She wanted to stand up but she could only get off the bed on the side facing Gabe, and she didn't want to get any closer to him.

Neither of them paid any attention to Jay and Diane, who were standing in the open doorway, shamelessly eavesdropping.

"You don't understand why I'm upset? Let me explain it to you," he said with awful calm. He'd moved to loom over the bed. "I went to sleep last night with a beautiful woman in my arms—a woman I've already said I love. I expected to wake up this morning with that same woman in my bed—or at least in my house. Instead I wake up to a polite little note that could have been written by a total stranger."

"It was a perfectly good note," she offered weakly. "I meant everything I said."

He made a noise that sounded suspiciously like a growl. "All debts paid in full," he quoted, his eyes flashing fire. "Did you mean that?"

"Yes," she admitted, wondering why he should be upset that she'd told him not to feel as if he owed her anything.

"Did you sleep with me because you thought you owed me something?" he roared.

Charity gaped at him, trying to see how he could have interpreted her note to mean that. She'd tried so hard to strike just the right balance.

"I...you didn't...I meant you shouldn't feel guilty anymore," she finally got out.

"Guilty! Is that all you think I feel?"

"I—" She looked past him at Diane, her eyes pleading for help. But Diane only gave her a completely unsympathetic grin, her eyes full of laughter. Charity was on her own.

"I think you felt very guilty about the shooting," she said carefully.

"Of course I felt guilty," he snapped. "Who wouldn't? But I've already told you—several times—that my feelings for you aren't guilt. I made love to you last night because I love you. What do I have to say to get that through your head?"

Charity saw Diane beaming with approval and she felt her own cheeks warm. So much for keeping her private life private. From the look on Gabe's face, she doubted he'd have cared if they were standing in the middle of the Rose Bowl.

"I never said you didn't like me," she began, her voice dropping.

"Like you? I love you, goddammit!" he barked in a less than loverlike tone. "At the moment I'm not sure I 'like' you at all."

Her heart began to thump. Despite herself, she almost believed him. Almost. But she had to be careful. She didn't think she could bear it if she let herself believe him and then found out he'd mistaken his feelings. Better never to have him than to lose him.

"It's easy to mistake guilt and . . . and affection for stronger emotions. I—Gabe!" His name was a startled shriek as he bent to grab her by the shoulders. Snatching her up off the bed, his mouth covered hers before she'd had time to regain her breath.

If Charity had wanted to resist, he didn't give her a chance. He put all his hunger and need into that kiss, and she was helpless to do anything but respond.

He ended as abruptly as he'd begun. Pulling his head back, he glared at her.

"Does that feel like guilt?" he snarled.

Charity could only stare at him, trying to gather her scattered wits. His eyes were still furious. And hurt, she realized suddenly. She'd hurt him. The realization was stunning. Gabe had always seemed so self-contained, as if nothing really got through to him. It had never occurred to her that she could hurt him. That he might care enough about her to be hurt.

That he might love her?

"Oh, what's the use," Gabe muttered, taking her continued silence as a confirmation that she didn't care. He released his hold on her shoulders, and Charity sank bonelessly to the bed, trying to absorb the incredible thought that he really did love her.

It was only when he turned away from the bed that she realized he was leaving. Walking out of her life. Because he thought she didn't care.

"Wait."

Wrapped in his own hurt, Gabe didn't even hear her husky plea. But Jay did. Acting with the presence of mind that made him an excellent doctor, he reached past Diane and grabbed hold of the doorknob, shutting the door in Gabe's face.

"What the hell?" Gabe stared at the closed door, wondering what sort of game Jay was playing. All he wanted was out of there. Charity had made it plain that she didn't love him. He'd gambled that she didn't realize the strength of her feelings, and he'd lost. Now he just wanted to go beat his head on a convenient telephone pole. He reached for the doorknob.

"Gabe." He stiffened but he didn't turn around. He didn't want to see her sympathetic look. No doubt it bothered her to think that she might have hurt him.

"Forget it," he said gruffly. He tugged on the doorknob, but something was holding the door shut. Something like Jay Baldwin, he guessed. Maybe instead of beating *his* head on a telephone pole, he'd beat Jay's head on one.

"Gabe, wait. Please."

Something in her voice reached him, breathing life into the hope he was sure was completely unfounded. He released the doorknob and turned toward her.

"What?"

She was standing next to the bed, and for just a moment he savored the miracle of seeing her on her feet. Even if he never saw her again, he'd at least know she was walking.

"I didn't mean to hurt you."

"No big deal." He shrugged.

"Gabe, are you sure you love me?"

My God, did she want to rub salt in the wounds? But there was something in her eyes that told him there was more than idle curiosity behind the question. Something he was afraid to believe in. He took a step toward her.

"I love you."

"And it's not guilt or pity or anything like that?"

"I'll always feel guilty that I hurt you, Charity. But I don't pity you. And I *do* know the difference between guilt and love."

She took a hesitant step forward, her fingers twisting in the hem of her nightshirt—a battered football jersey emblazoned with a giant number one.

"I'm walking again now, and it won't be long before I'll be able to go back to work and get an apartment. You don't have to worry about me or wonder if I can get along." She seemed anxious that he understand just how well she could get along without him.

"I'm glad. But that doesn't change the way I feel about you."

"You're sure? Really, really sure?" she whispered, her heart in her eyes.

"I'm really, really sure." He stopped inches away. "I love you, Charity. Whether you ever walked or not, I love you."

"Oh." Interpreting that, quite correctly, to mean that she felt the same, Gabe caught her in his arms. "It's just that I couldn't stand it if you changed your mind," she said, her voice muffled against his shirt.

"I'm not going to change my mind." He slid one hand into her hair, tilting her head back until her eyes met his. "Are *you* sure? You're not feeling that you owe me something for taking care of you?"

"No. I'm sure."

"You might tell me just what it is you're sure of."
His smile had a wistful edge. Looking into his eyes,
Charity saw a touch of uncertainty, and she realized
suddenly that he was just as worried about her feelings as she had been about his. Her arms tightened
around him, and she had to swallow a lump in her
throat before she could get her voice out.

"I love you, Gabriel London. I love you. I love—"
Gabe's mouth smothered her words. There'd be
time enough later to tell her he'd left the force, time
enough to talk about Wyoming. They had the rest of
their lives.

♦ H A R L E Q U I N ®

A Calendar of Romance

Be a part of American Romance's year-long celebration of love and the holidays of 1992. Celebrate those special times each month with your favorite authors.

Next month, it's an explosion of springtime flowers and new beginnings in

		APRIL				
S	M	T	W	T	F	S
			1	2	3	4
5	6	7	8	9	10	11
12	13	14	15	16	17	18
19	20	21	22	23	24	25
	27	28	29	30		

#433 A MAN FOR EASTER
by Stella Cameron

Read all the books in *A Calendar of Romance*, coming to you one per month, all year, only in American Romance.

Following the success of WITH THIS RING,
Harlequin cordially invites you to enjoy the
romance of the wedding season with

BARBARA BRETTON
RITA CLAY ESTRADA
SANDRA JAMES
DEBBIE MACOMBER

A collection of romantic stories that celebrate the joy,
excitement, and mishaps of planning that special day
by these four award-winning Harlequin authors.

**Available in April at your favorite Harlequin
retail outlets.**

THTH

Take 4 bestselling love stories FREE

Plus get a FREE surprise gift!